Polestar

A Global Paranormal Security Agency Story

Jodi Kendrick

SoulGate Publishing

Dragon Island
Dragon Heat

Enchanted Ardor
Wish

EveL Worlds : FUCN'A
Tough Nut
Diamond in the Ruff
Honeyed Nut
Gorilla in the Hiss
FUCN'A Collection One
Pedigree Collection

Finely Aged
Dragon Steel

Global Paranormal Security Agency
Awakened
Surfacing
Polestar
Aquatic Investigations
Prowler

The Kindred Chronicles
Healer
Mercenary

The Soaring Dragon Chronicles
Return Flight
Changeling

The Global Paranormal Security Agency

The Global Paranormal Security Agency is a hidden investigative group dedicated to bridging the paranormal and human worlds in an effort to keep everyone safe.

Protect. Defend. Seek Justice.

***Thank you*!**

To my family, friends and writing community. Your continued love, support and encouragement keep me going. Without you, I'd still be dabbling and drifting.

Jessica Ripley – So many projects to keep me out of trouble!

To **John & Kevin** for their patience and invaluable feedback. To **Kim** for her keen eye and editorial work to keep me looking spiffy!

For Jess R.

ONE

ANALIESE ORTEGA'S EYES SNAPPED open, heart still racing from her nightmare. She blinked, scanning the dark room for what had startled her awake.

Bzht. Bzht. Bzht.

She blew out her breath and reached for her phone as reality replaced the nightmare.

"Carson," she mumbled, rolling onto her back, rubbing her face with her free hand. She didn't bother asking if he knew what time it was, because he wouldn't be calling at a ridiculous hour if it weren't necessary.

"There's a chartered plane waiting for you at Santa Ana airport."

"I hate that airport."

"It's close."

"I'm not ready."

There was a long silence before Carson answered. "I know. I'm sorry about Antony, but we need you, Ana."

"Farida can do it."

"On assignment in New Zealand."

She struggled to think of another agent from the Global Paranormal Security Agency that could take her place.

Some other objections.

Set by her bedside, her gaze found the only photo of Antony she couldn't let go of.

Pain twisted her heart.

My fault.

She shoved the sensation away, locking down her emotions.

Carson continued. "The data from our informant is paying off, Ana. We have a lead." He paused. "You've been there from the start. I know you want to see this case through."

Dammit. I do.

Ana threw off her duvet. Her feet hit the cool floor and propelled her toward the patio doors of her bedroom, over-looking the beach.

The surf rushed in and rolled out. Once more.

"I need to shower and pack."

"The pilot will wait, but don't keep him waiting too long. He gets grumpy."

"Noted."

"Pack warm."

"Why? Where am I going?" She spun around, eyes finding her closet door.

"Iceland."

"Iceland! Carson, you know I hate cold places."

"Don't we all." He sighed.

"Just don't have Lirikai pick me up when I arrive. My nerves can't handle her driving."

Carson chuckled, "She misses you."

"Carson, please."

"Don't worry, your ride is already taken care of. Besides, Lirikai is working elsewhere at the moment."

Oh, thank God.

"You know I like her—I really do."

"I know."

She could hear the mirth in his voice.

"She's just..."

"Intense."

"Yes. Intense."

"Her driving is improving."

Ana grunted. Carson laughed.

She hung up the phone, then tossed it onto the foot of her bed as she straightened the duvet and fluffed the pillows. Opening the sliding glass door, she stepped onto her balcony, breathing deeply of the sea air, giving herself a few moments to fully awaken.

And absorb the warm California air.

She'd be going to the boardroom for a briefing first, so office wear.

North.

She'd have to dig deep into her closet.

Do I even own cold weather clothes?

Her shoulders drooped. She'd have to layer. A lot.

I hate the cold.

I'm not ready for this.

Ana allowed herself a few more moments to reconcile. Carson needed her.

Ready or not, people's lives are at stake.

"Right then, no time to waste."

MAGNUS BJORNSON YAWNED, PACING the tarmac outside of his chartered plane.

He glanced at his watch again.

"An hour late," he growled.

Refueled, the plane waited. He'd already been through all the checks. Twice. He didn't mind long hours in the cockpit, but disliked unnecessary added time. Especially when a storm was expected between himself and the landing site. This extra wait time could cost them more than just an hour at the other end of the journey.

He sighed and went into the hangar office to make coffee.

About to take his first sip of the hot brew, rapid footsteps amid the sound of rolling wheels drew his attention to a tiny brunette dressed for a boardroom, hauling two suitcases. She could have fit into either of them with space to spare.

The coffee was too hot, but he drank some anyway as he observed the hangar official with his passenger.

It was going to be a long flight.

He considered the rest of the brew, gulped it down, and tossed the paper cup in the trash bin.

"I'm already late. Please tell the pilot I'm here and we can take off right away—unless someone else is traveling with me? Is anyone else expected?"

"No ma'am. Just you."

Her narrow shoulders lowered a fraction. "Okay, just watch that one doesn't roll away while I bring this one up." She motioned toward the bright teal case as she tightened her grip on the lime green one.

"But madam, I can take those for you. Just leave it here."

"No, it's okay, I've got it," she insisted, dragging it up the first step as though she were a champion weightlifter pulling a maxed bar.

Magnus smirked.

He patted the official's shoulder as he moved toward the steps locked below the opening and grabbed the case with one hand, then mounted and grabbed the second case with the other.

"No, it's okay, really, I—Oh." She said, when she turned to stare into Magnus' face, who still stood taller than her despite being lower on the steps. Her gaze shot down to his easy grasp of her oversized luggage.

"You should go in," he suggested.

"I really could take one."

"I insist. We're already late."

"Right. Okay." She nodded and scurried up the steps and into the charter.

Magnus sighed as he followed.

I bet everything she owns is in these two cases.

She reappeared in the door, preparing to descend again.

"Agent Ortega?"

"I forgot my laptop bag by the front door."

Thankfully, the official had noted the oversight and was already trotting back with the bag.

"Thank you so much." She smiled and disappeared inside.

Deciding to ignore the dimples her cheeks made when she smiled, Magnus secured the cases in the back, then did final checks as he moved toward the cockpit.

"Is the pilot ready?" Agent Ortega asked, fastening her seat-belt.

"He is," Magnus said, closing and securing the door. He nodded to the official below.

"But I didn't see him up front." She glanced toward the back of the plane.

"I'm the pilot," Magnus said, stepping into the cockpit. "Anything else I can do for you before we get on our way?"

She blinked.

"Uhm. No. Thank you," she said. "Sorry about all the luggage. Perenga said 'pack warm' and I panicked a bit. I don't like the cold."

Magnus grunted. "You get used to it. Wheels up in ten. Stow your bag." He nodded to the laptop bag on the seat beside her.

"Of course."

Magnus wasn't fazed. He was familiar with the expression of disbelief due to his appearance.

Six foot five, impeccably kept long hair and beard, Nirvana t-shirt and jeans. No, he didn't dress like a pilot. Nor did he think he had to in order to do his job properly.

Although, the agency often tried to convince him otherwise.

Agent Ortega clearly adhered to the agency's dress protocol in her crisp office skirt-suit, white button-up and heels.

No wonder she's so uptight. No room to breathe.

As he cast her one last glance, he noticed she had retrieved an eye mask from her laptop satchel before tucking the bag beneath her seat.

He closed the door and got to work.

TWO

ANALIESE LURCHED AT THE sensation of falling in darkness, then skipping over a series of speed bumps at racetrack speed.

Her heart hammered wildly, and her limbs flailed, slamming against too-close objects.

Chest heaving, her hands clutched the arms of her chair as soon as she found them, then she reached up and ripped the mask off her eyes to dispel the nightmare.

Plane. Charter. Giant pilot. Going to Iceland.

Had she slept the entire flight? She glanced at her watch, then pushed the window shade up.

Chaos filled the small window.

Rain poured down the glass. The plane swayed. The steel-tinted sky lit with a flash, followed by a deafening crash.

Ana slammed the window screen shut, then threw herself back against her seat, eyes closed as she prayed. Her fingers gripped the seat handles, feet securely against the plane floor.

Her gaze darted to the small door, blocking her view to the pilot. This particular plane had a thin wall dividing the cockpit from the rest of the cabin. Probably to stop passengers, like herself, from screaming at the pilot in terror.

A dull 'pong' drew her attention to the ceiling.

The pilot had illuminated the seatbelt sign.

No shit.

The plane lurched and continued to descend.

Breath stuttered through her chest. One of her nails cracked as her grip tightened on the seat.

She hated flying almost as much as she hated the cold.

"If I die... in a plane crash... in the North Atlantic... I'm going to friggin' haunt you, Carson Perenga," she spat through her clenched teeth.

She was almost sorry for all the complaining she'd done while at the mercy of Lirikai's driving. Almost.

At least, in that case, she was already on the ground.

She waited for the 'brace for impact' message to come over the com. Instead, the plane leveled out and eased downward. She held her breath till the wheels touched the ground and they rolled to a stop. The seatbelt sign went dark, then the engine went silent.

Ana disengaged her nails from her seat and unbuckled her belt, still cursing Carson's name.

The scowling giant pilot squeezed through the cockpit door. "Slight delay in plans. We'll stop here to ride out the storm."

"We're not at our destination? Where are we?" Ana shoved the window blind back up again, now that it was safe to look outside. There was nothing but rain-lashed barren rockscape pockmarked with small bodies of water between a few stubborn trees.

We're nowhere.

"Fogo Island." His expression remained unchanged.

She wracked her geographical memory, trying to recall where Fogo was as she stared at the pilot.

"Newfoundland," he provided, then turned toward the exterior door to release the steps. "We departed a little bit late, and the storm arrived a little bit early, so here we are."

Ana recalled Carson's warning on the phone *'The pilot will wait, but don't keep him waiting too long. He gets grumpy.'*

She'd only been an hour late. It had taken her that long to find all her 'winter' gear and choose the right shoes for the office. Carson had neglected to tell her if she needed field or boardroom wear for the duration of the case. She had to be ready for anything. And she was currently dressed for the office. Not a frigid rainstorm off the coast of apocalypse-scape.

"Where are we going?" She pulled the edges of her thin jacket close as a gust of wind wound through the cabin once the door was open.

"Out." He descended the steps.

Ana found a large hand extended through the open door to help her down the steps.

The pilot's bear-like grasp was warm as it engulfed her hand. She gasped. Her fingers felt as though she'd inserted them into a warm energy current. Images flashed through her mind's eye, too rapid to grasp before she could throw her barriers up to block the transfer of energetic information.

She descended quickly, sliding past his trim torso to the tarmac, trying to shake the sudden onslaught of images and sensations.

Ana grit her teeth trying to control the influx of information.

I'm never going to get used to that.

He gestured toward a squat building, indicating she should enter. Trotting forward, she glanced back to see that he was securing the plane, impervious to the rain soaking his clothes.

The door was locked, so she waited under the narrow overhang, holding her jacket closed, shivering as rainwater dribbled down her bare legs to pool in the toes of her office pumps.

She'd expected to be chauffeured to an office like Maeda's—or her own, for that matter.

Ah. Field work.

She sighed. She would soon find out if this was worse than Odson Blackridge's mountain cabin. She prayed that this facility at least had running water and an indoor toilet. Cell service would be nice.

Though, as she peered through the driving rain and saw absolutely nothing, she had her doubts.

Finally, the pilot strode in her direction, unhurried by the downpour. She blinked at the alluring vision of the tall man, t-shirt plastered to a mountain range of muscle and valley. Withdrawing a key ring from his jeans pocket, he unlocked the door and gestured for her to precede him.

Shivering, she darted inside the black interior.

A few seconds later, lights flickered on. "No customs agent on duty?" she asked through chattering teeth.

"Private runway. They know our tags and leave us alone." He strode across the open space of the small hangar toward an office door set in the wall between a work bench and a large tool chest. "I'll radio in to let them know we're grounded for the time being."

Radio.

No cell service.

Damn.

Ana followed him through the door.

"Oh, thank God!" she blurted on seeing a bathroom door, and rushed toward it. After the stress of that unexpected landing and the icy rain, Ana had a sudden emergency of her own.

MAGNUS' GAZE TRAILED THE pint-sized agent as she bee-lined for the lavatory and slammed the door shut.

He sighed and made his way toward the kitchenette to fill and set the kettle to boil before powering on the radio.

He contacted Joey Kane, his superior, confirming his position and status. They'd continue on as soon as the storm let up—with a change of destination.

Negotiations weren't going as smoothly as Kane had hoped.

"Sorry to do this, Magnus. We need Agent Ortega's skills on this, but until we resolve this disagreement, we need to delay revealing too much to our *partners*."

"Understood. An extended journey it is, then."

He switched off the radio and returned to the kitchen to pull mugs from the cupboard.

The agent approached, rubbing her hands together, shivering in her damp jacket.

Magnus poured water over the tea, handed her a mug, then went to fetch a space heater from the utility closet. "Sit over there." He set the heater on the floor next to the chair and plugged it in.

She followed his instruction, grasping the mug with both hands. "How much further to Iceland from here?"

"We're not going to Iceland. Ireland."

"No, I'm pretty sure we're going to Iceland. I wouldn't confuse 'pack warm' for frigid Iceland with Ireland. Ever."

"Plan's changed."

"Since when? Why?" Agent Ortega jumped to her feet, still clutching her mug.

"Since the order came when I radioed in."

"What's going on?"

Magnus shrugged.

Agent Ortega scowled at him. "Listen, Mister—what's your name?"

"Bjornson. Magnus Bjornson."

"Of course it is. Look at you," she muttered. "Mr. Bjornson. *My* orders were to meet my team in Iceland. I packed for Iceland. Two very large suitcases. For Iceland. Until I can confirm that *my* orders have changed. You will fly me to Iceland."

He lifted a brow, looking down at the bossy woman shivering in front of him with a pink nose. "Agent Bjornson," he corrected, leaning over her. "Your orders depend on mine. And I have just been told to fly you to Ireland. So unless you want to walk around this little island in the driving rain to find your own ride, you will accompany me to Ireland."

She sniffed, bright spots appearing on her tanned cheeks. "And how much longer do I have to *fly* with you? If that's what you call flying? What was *that,* anyway? I think I lost ten years of my life in that landing."

Magnus stiffened. "That maneuvering saved your life. Had you arrived *as expected*, we'd have missed that storm and be nearly to Iceland by now. Then someone *else* could have flown you on to Ireland now that the plan has changed."

When she opened her mouth to speak, she swayed on her feet. Magnus grasped her wrist to steady her.

She gasped and dropped her mug as her eyes rolled back.

The mug hit the concrete floor with a crash as Magnus jerked her forward toward himself to stop her from falling backward. "Agent Ortega?"

He caught her as she slumped against him. Her head lolled; eyes closed. While supporting her, he checked her vitals and eased her into the chair.

What's wrong with her?

"Agent Ortega?" he said again, easing her back into the chair. "Ortega?" His hands swept her forehead and cheeks. Her skin was pale despite her pink tipped nose and rosy cheeks.

Magnus swept her slight form into his arms and carried her into the small bunk room, tucked away beyond the kitchenette. Gently laying Agent Ortega on the cot, he pulled off her shoes. Her bare feet and calves were wet and cold. He eased her upright so he could remove the soaked jacket. The thin silk blouse beneath clung to her damp skin, outlining the contours of her lacy bra.

"Shit."

Easing her head back onto the small pillow, he went to fetch the space heater, to plug it in next to the cot. He cranked the knob, so that the filaments ticked as they grew to bright hot orange. It wasn't heating the room fast enough.

"It's not even winter. How can anyone catch a chill so damned fast?" he grumbled, rubbing her arms and legs to warm them up while the heater worked to bring the room temperature up.

The sensation of her silky skin beneath his palms didn't go unnoticed, just ignored.

Trembles wracked her body.

Quickly, Magnus unbuttoned her blouse, peeling it from her skin to drape it over a couple of hooks screwed to the wall next to the door. Then he pulled his own t-shirt up over his head.

Dragging a chair from the office, he sat, then carefully pulled Ortega onto his lap. He wrapped his arms around her lean form, ensuring her back was pressed to his chest. After a few moments, the trembling eased.

"Antony." She sighed, easing her head back onto his shoulder.

As soon as he was sure the agent could maintain body heat on her own, Magnus slid her back onto the cot, pulling the blanket around her shoulders and torso, then moved to rub the warmth into her feet and ankles.

The electric heater continued to tick furiously, working hard to warm the concrete and steel room.

After about ten minutes, Magnus went back to the plane, bare chested, to fetch one of the agent's suitcases. When he returned to the hangar, he left Ortega's suitcase at the foot of the cot, grabbed his wet shirt, and draped it over the back of the chair, pulling it back into the office.

Retrieving his own mug of tea, he sat down, impervious to the cool air. As a polar bear shifter, the cold didn't bother him.

He positioned his chair so that he could see Agent Ortega through the open door. She was a burrito on the thin cot. Her dark hair framed her small, round face, making her look younger than she probably was. And vulnerable, which she probably wasn't.

The only sounds were the steady ticking of the heater over the howling wind driving the rain against the steel roof of the airstrip hangar.

In the morning, he'd refuel the plane and get his new colleague to Ireland.

It would have been easier putting her on a commercial flight, but Kane had insisted that Ortega arrive as soon as possible, hence the private charter.

Magnus rubbed a hand over his face. Whatever they needed her for, it was important. Given their verbal exchange before she passed out, the sooner he delivered her, the better for both of them.

He didn't appreciate anyone slamming his flying skills, not even a feisty little agent from the Global Paranormal Security Agency.

THREE

ANA WATCHED THE LANDSCAPE through the same small window of her plane seat.

The Irish coast was beautiful. And green.

Not the north, as she'd worked herself up for.

She stifled a yawn and glanced toward the closed cockpit door concealing her giant pilot.

Ana's thoughts returned to the moment she'd awakened to discover that she was half naked and burrowed into an uncomfortable cot next to a blazing space heater. Then, unexpectedly, had taken in a full view of her pilot dozing bare-chested on an office chair in the next room. His long, long, jean-clad legs braced the chair against the wall behind him where his head rested. His large hands lay clasped over his belt buckle.

Her eyes trailed over the tattoos adorning the muscle. On the small table next to him were the remnants of the mug he'd given her the night before. She frowned, unable to recall anything after... what? What had happened?

God, she couldn't remember anything beyond feeling so damned cold.

And here she sat, flying to Ireland.

Bjornson, he'd said his name was. Agent? Yes, Agent Magnus Bjornson.

Tall, blond, and silent. He was a shifter of some kind. She'd gleaned that much from the unintentional contact.

He'd barely said anything to her since he caught her staring at him from her little bundle on the cot where she'd slept. As he seemed to have slept all night on an office chair.

She sighed.

What stupid shit did I say last night?

All she could piece together was the recollection of feeling... but it was gone again before she could grasp it.

Her heightened anxiety made chaos of her emotional barrier. The self-control that her boss, Jack Maeda, had been working to help her hone was rice paper thin. And with all the rain and the wind, being called to duty, and the storm forcing the plane down, it had all just torn through.

She glanced at the door again. Had Agent Bjornson touched her? If he had, she didn't recall it, and normally she did.

Sometimes, when all her barriers became depleted, the slightest touch could bring her to her knees with information overload. But it would stay with her, like an echo chamber, until she could snatch every piece and categorize it.

This was different.

Her vision had gone blinding white. Then she fell into darkness.

Emotions, thoughts, impressions. None were tangible. Not enough. Too much.

Either way, she decided that until she had better control over her channeling, she wouldn't touch him again.

Not that she *should* touch him again, because she *shouldn't*.

Although, part of her secretly wished she could remember if he had touched her at all.

Ana's cheeks burned as images of all those tattooed muscles rolled through her brain, where the psychic impressions wouldn't.

She cleared her suddenly dry throat.

For the best.

I prefer clean-cut men; she reminded herself. *Like Antony...* her heart crumbled at the reminder.

Antony's smiling face rose in her mind's eye, blotting out everything else, followed by his other expressions. Confusion over her explanations of her work. Resolve when he'd ended their long-term relationship. Fear over her insistent warnings that something was wrong. Pity when he left on his voyage out to sea. Routine training exercise.

The end of her world loomed with his disappearance.

She shut down the rest with a deep, deep breath and turned her focus back to the window.

This was her life now.

She'd always been devoted to her work at the GPSA. And after so many recent heartbreaking experiences, it was her life's work now.

No time for distractions, like attractive Viking-ish pilots, or dead relationships.

Her grandmother had warned her.

Ana hadn't listened.

She was listening now.

The plane descended the last few hundred feet. She barely felt the wheels graze the tarmac as they coasted to a smooth stop.

Much better than last night's landing.

Agent Bjornson emerged from the small cockpit door once he parked the plane and turned the engines off.

With her laptop bag slung over her back, Ana was already trying to free her suitcases from the aft baggage compartment. She glanced back as he opened the door hatch and lowered the steps.

A moment later, his large hand hovered over hers, straining on the suitcase handle. "Go."

"But I can get this one—."

He grunted, and she moved aside, surprised by his gruff non-verbal order.

She huffed, slid past him, and exited the plane.

They were on another private landing strip with an accompanying office and hangar.

Fine. If Agent Bjornson wanted to be her baggage handler, so be it.

Her conscience pinged her.

What was wrong with her?

He'd helped her last night. Maybe she had awakened shirtless, but she'd also been bundled onto a cot with a blasting space heater while the man had slept on a frikking office chair in a cold room.

Don't be an asshole, Ana. Get your shit together and mind your manners.

"Thank you," she said as he approached, exposed biceps flexed, carrying her cases like two shopping bags.

His second grunt sounded something like *'welcome'*, but she couldn't be sure. He didn't head toward the office door as expected, but veered toward the side of the small building and a parked car.

At the car, he stopped, reached into his pocket, and pressed a button on a universal key fob. Releasing the trunk hatch, he tossed the cases into it and closed it.

Agent Bjornson opened the front door on the left of the vehicle, rounded the car, and got in on the right.

She sighed. He was her chauffeur, too.

Settled in next to him and belted, she leaned toward the door to create more space between them.

She didn't want any more accidental readings. She couldn't manage it while she wasn't in full control of her abilities. "Where are we going?"

"Kane Estate."

Ana sucked in a breath.

GPSA Headquarters.

This was more important than she thought.

MAGNUS GLANCED AT HIS passenger while navigating the car up the long drive toward the manor house. He ignored the circular path, steering the car around the back toward the carriage house's converted garage. Pressing a button to open the door, he parked the car, retrieved Agent Ortega's baggage, and led the way through the back halls of the house.

Ortega's heels clicked a staccato behind him as she kept pace with his long strides.

Mentally, he grumbled over her sharp accusations about the integrity of his flight skills.

He quashed the temptation to lengthen his strides and increase his pace.

Thankfully, she maintained her silence.

"Magnus! Give the girl a break!" Agent Raya Burns' voice echoed up the hall. "You're making her run a marathon in heels with the pace you're setting, man."

Magnus halted, swinging around, narrowly missing Ortega with the life-size suitcases, to see Burns' head poking out of a side room they'd just passed.

"No worries... Burns... I can keep up. Good to see you again, by the way... And thanks for the replacement shoes," Ortega said between gasps.

Magnus rolled his eyes, set the luggage down, and back-tracked to speak to Burns. "Maeda?"

"Kane's office," Burns said to Magnus. Her gaze swung back to Ortega. "They fit?"

Ortega gave Burns a thumbs up as she rubbed a stitch in her side.

Magnus sighed. "How long have they been there?"

"Couple hours. Ortega's room is in the east wing across from mine."

A couple of hours? Not good. Not surprising, but not good.

He grunted, retrieved the bags, and resumed his quest to deposit Ortega in her room and get on with the investigation they'd gathered for.

"I can do that," Ortega called after him. "I told him I can carry my own luggage." He heard her say to Burns.

Burns snorted. "There's no elevator in this place. Hey Magnus, she has a sweet face but don't let her touch you with her woo-woo hands or she'll steal all your secrets."

"My woo-woo—" Ortega huffed. "Funny."

The clicking heels also resumed behind Magnus, catching up to him shortly after rounding the corner and thankfully turned to dull, rapid thuds when he cut through the study for the service stairs.

Finally, he deposited her bags outside the room Burns had mentioned.

"This place is incredible," Ortega said, stopping next to her bags.

He gestured toward her door.

"Thank you," she said, looking up at him. "Really. For getting me here and hauling my bags." She stuck her hand out in front of his midsection.

The corner of his mouth twitched at the professional gesture after their last *interesting* twenty-four hours together.

Burns' words about woo-woo hands echoed back to him. Whatever that meant. Besides, the only secrets he had that she could steal from him were about his work, and she was already here for that.

Accepting the handshake, the firm effort she put into it surprised him.

"There is a house manager if you need anything. There are phones in the rooms, like in hotels. Since Kane and Maeda are still in a meeting, I'm sure you'll have a bit of time before they send someone for you."

She nodded, not making any effort to go into her room.

"Anything else?"

She bit her lip. "Just an apology." She blew out her breath. "For being so rude last night—"

He lifted a hand to stop her words. "Forgotten. See you around."

He spun away as she drew breath to say something else, and walked away before she could. At the end of the corridor, he opened the door to his own room. Glancing back, he noted Ortega was struggling with the second of her two suitcases.

And Perenga wanted to send this woman to Iceland? The man was losing his faculties after gods only knew how many centuries he'd spent in this planet's oceans. If Ortega could be afflicted with hypothermia from a rainstorm, she'd never survive actual cold weather.

Or maybe they'd redirected the plane here because Perenga realized how much of a mistake sending that woman into the frigid landscape would be.

He shrugged, pulled his shirt off, balled it up and threw it into a hamper as he strode toward his shower.

Not my problem.

I did my job. Now she's Perenga and Burns' problem.

As he stepped under the steaming water, he couldn't help but recall the sensation of her vulnerable body balled up on his lap, shivering in his arms. Her silky-smooth skin smelled of California sunshine, vanilla coconut, and a scent that was uniquely hers.

He blinked away that wreck of a thought-train, snatched the soap from the shelf and began lathering.

She's not my type, anyway.

Magnus was used to women who had a powerful presence, could hold their own on a physical level, and wouldn't fly away with a sneeze.

But, if he was honest with himself, as he usually was, he grudgingly admired her stubborn determination to handle those ridiculous suitcases herself.

Adorable.

And those dimples... when she actually smiled.

Magnus snorted and turned his back to the water stream.

Despite her tantrum, she'd never acted as though anyone ought to serve her. Quite the opposite. He attributed the poor behavior to fear and fever right before she passed out.

He frowned, recalling Burns' words again.

What the hell does that even mean?

He shook away the thought after trying to reconcile the weird statement with the pretty round face, pert little nose over full, pillowy lips.

Soft.

He was sure of it.

He grunted away the thought, glanced down and sighed, noting the erection that told him just how soft he thought Ortega's lips were.

That wouldn't do.

He faced the hot stream again and cranked the faucet, blasting himself with frigid water.

No. That wouldn't do at all.

FOUR

ANA PERCHED ON THE edge of an elegant, silk-embroidered chair stuffed with horsehair, in the most luxurious eighteenth-century library she'd ever been in.

Barely aware she was present, Jolena Kane and Jack Maeda still argued by the floor-to-ceiling French doors overlooking a rolling green that ended some distance away at a dark band of woods. Their coffees, in hand, were also forgotten except to use as emphasis on certain points.

Ana sighed and sipped her own drink. By now, they were on their third iteration of the same debate. Apparently, they'd forgotten her, too, despite her being summoned almost as soon as she'd closed the door to her room after hauling her suitcases in.

Two full-sized suitcases. What was she thinking?

I panicked.

With nothing else to do, she carried on in the theme of the moment and ignited an internal argument with herself over every moment since Carson Perenga's call woke her with the word 'Iceland'.

She shivered and sipped more of her hot coffee.

To a lifelong California girl, images of Iceland evoked frigid, barren landscapes of rock, snow, and ice. Sure, the northern lights would be pretty, but the light show wasn't worth the risk of frostbite.

So, she'd packed almost everything she had in her closet that could be considered colder weather wear. That done, she reminded herself that the routine was to be summoned to your superior's office for a briefing, settled into a hotel to review the file and freshen up before getting to work the following morning.

Pretty much like what was happening now. Here, in Ireland. Not Iceland.

Not for her, just yet, anyhow.

"Look, we were barely able to squeak that ship out of territorial waters before their coast guard arrived," Kane said to Maeda.

"Perenga and McLachlan know what they're doing. They can handle themselves in the deep-sea sectors. It's Ortega I'm worried about."

Ana's gaze snapped to the director. He scowled at Kane, his superior.

"Noted. That's why she's here, instead." Kane's attention flicked to Ana. She turned, finally drank from her cup, and set the vessel on a nearby gilt end table before moving toward her.

Ana set her own cup aside, careful not to rattle the porcelain, and stood to face Kane at eye level. Well, almost at eye level, the other woman stood several inches taller than she did.

"It's good to see you again, Agent," Kane said, extending her hand.

Ana shook it. "Thank you, Madam Kane."

"Feel free to call me Joey, here at the estate. Jack's been keeping me apprised of your progress on this case."

Ana nodded. "I've been working with the rescued survivors and Raya Burns during debriefings when she returns from the field."

"But you've been on leave for the last month."

Ana swallowed. Nodded. "Yes."

Kane's expression softened a fraction. "I was sorry to hear about Private Antony Ruiz. Please accept my condolences and those of the other members of the Organization."

"Thank you, ma'am. We had already separated before... before our team cracked the Montreal trafficking sector. But still on friendly terms until... well, until a few days leading up to the accident."

Kane nodded. "It's hard losing someone you love. And it hasn't been long." She glanced at Maeda. "Your director insists you need more time, Ortega. I ordered Perenga to call you in, despite Maeda's protests."

Ana looked at Maeda's grim expression. He wasn't a soft man. Professional and demanding, often setting Ana through grueling exercises to hone her ability so she could be a stronger tool for the GPSA. People's lives depended on all their abilities to go above and beyond what even the most skilled human agents could do.

Maeda knew what Ana's capabilities were. She respected him to no end.

He was also the only person who knew what had happened, and how deep Antony's loss went.

Ana straightened her spine and shoulders. She'd told Perenga she wasn't ready.

"People's lives are at stake," she finally said.

It wasn't really a choice. She had to set her personal grief and guilt aside.

She went on, "You mentioned a ship, so there are more survivors. When do I talk to them?"

"I had Magnus bring you here instead of Iceland because we've run into jurisdictional resistance, so we have other agents working on that. The ship is being escorted to the north coast where the survivors will disembark. We're working with Garda and the Irish Coast Guard. They know we're a branch of Interpol, but nothing more. They'll care for the survivors and provide us with access to interview them."

"Can I get aboard the ship?"

"I'll make it happen," Kane said, "Maeda is going to consolidate the data and draw up a new plan of action. We're getting close, and any of these survivors could hold the key to where that trafficking hub is located."

"I know. I'll do everything I can." She glanced at Maeda, whose expression hadn't changed as he watched her.

She swallowed. She didn't need to be psychic to sense his disapproval.

"You'll go first thing in the morning. I'd prefer to be there when they disembark, but Garda will want to have their medical needs attended to before we can have them. Magnus Bjornson, Raya Burns and Aaron Connor are your primary team on this." Kane studied Ana's face for a long moment. "I know you're the right person for this case, Ana. That's my superpower." Kane's lips quirked.

Ana's shoulders eased a fraction. "Yes, ma'am."

"Get some rest. There won't be much time for it in the coming days."

"I'll walk you back to your room," Maeda said, striding toward the mahogany paneled door to open it for her. He led her along a different path from what she'd seen before, and she wondered if she'd have the time to get to know the estate's secrets before she went home.

If I go home.

She sucked in a breath at the unexpected thought, but it was true. As a field agent, there was always the danger that one of the team wouldn't make it home.

"Kane's right," she said to Maeda's back as she followed him.

He glanced back over his shoulder. "I don't know that she's right, but she's not wrong."

Ana snorted. "Cryptic as ever."

He slowed his brisk pace. "You know what I mean."

"I know, but we don't have a choice."

He stopped walking. She stopped to face him.

"If your emotions block your ability—."

"I know. And I told Carson I wasn't ready. How can I be?" her voice cracked, "My ability was useless to save Antony and his crew, Jack. I tried to warn him, and it made no difference. He died. They all died anyway. How can I trust that? I thought he could save them if he just knew—." She swallowed down anymore words.

Jack nodded. He understood. He always did.

She'd been having nightmares since the accident. A routine naval exercise gone wrong. Antony and his crew were never recovered from the ocean.

Controlling her grief, she straightened. "But I have to at least try. Any information I can glean is better than no information. You said so when you started training me."

"As long as you can allow enough information in to interpret it correctly and not let your personal emotions taint it."

He resumed walking. Ana followed until they arrived back at her door again.

"Go through the practices tonight. Rest and find your balance."

"Thanks, Jack. For everything."

"You're a good agent, Ana. I know you need more time. Anyone would after a loss like that. But, yes, time is essential, and we need you." He rubbed a hand over his cleanly shaved scalp. "I'll see you in the morning before you leave," he said, and departed back the way they'd come.

She watched him till he rounded the corner and turned back to her door. Hand on the knob, she glanced to the other end of the hall, where she'd seen Magnus go earlier.

Is that his room?

Memories of Magnus Bjornson over the last twenty-four hours flickered through her mind. She was going to be working directly with him.

She twisted the doorknob and entered her room.

Shower first, then practice.

I have no time to waste on thoughts of bearish pilots that smell nice. *Really* nice.

AT THE SOUND OF hurried footsteps, Magnus glanced up from pouring his coffee into a travel mug.

Agent *Ortega, no doubt.*

Seconds later, the woman in question entered through the open door of the breakfast room.

Today she wore a pantsuit and more reasonable shoes.

Her dark hair tumbled down so that it framed her face, making her dark eyes look larger in her small face.

She straightened her shoulders and breezed toward the spread of croissants, scones, muffins, and pastries he had no names for.

The scent that was uniquely hers, mingled with coconut and vanilla, drifted past his nose.

"Good morning," she mumbled, reaching for the raspberry jam and a scone. "Not hungry?"

"Nope." Magnus had eaten a full breakfast between his six a.m. run around the estate grounds, first in his human form, then in his animal form, and a morning shower. His coffee in hand was, in fact, his third of the day—so far.

Studying her down-turned face, he noted the concealer powdered across the delicate skin below her eyes as she stifled a yawn.

Raya Burns' laughter echoed in the corridor before she appeared in the door, followed by another familiar face.

Magnus smiled at his teammates. "Nice to see you up before noon, Connor."

"That's *Agent* Connor to you, Bjornson. And you should try it, you know. You could use the extra hours' beauty rest."

Magnus snorted.

Connor turned to Agent Ortega, proffering a hand. "Aaron Connor."

"Analiese Ortega. Stationed on the West Coast—California," she added as she accepted Connor's hand with a wide smile.

Magnus sipped his coffee as he observed her friendly interaction with Connor.

She hadn't smiled at *him* like that, although she *had* offered her hand as a professional courtesy.

The fine bones of her slim fingers had all but disappeared in his grasp.

Unbidden, he recalled the sensation of her smooth skin under his palm as he tended her unconscious form at the hangar. He cleared his throat, shoving the image of his vulnerable colleague from his mind, and sipped more coffee.

"I see you brought the boots I sent you," Burns said to Ortega.

"You sent Ortega boots? You've never sent me boots, and we've been working together for years," Connor complained.

Mischief glinted in Ortega's eye as the corner of her mouth quirked. "Well, the incident involved a mountain forest run and a taser." She shrugged her narrow shoulders. "Burns owed me."

"Come on, Ortega. What happens on the mountain, stays on the mountain," Burns growled.

Magnus chuckled, recalling Burns' report of events that led Ortega and Perenga to working with their team. "I'm impressed. No one has ever tased Burns before."

"Shit, you must be fast with that thing," Connor said, looking from Ortega to Burns.

"Fast and fierce when it comes to my favorite boots," Ortega said, biting into her scone.

Burns grabbed a couple of pieces of fruit. "I heard Lirikai owes you a new skirt."

"She does. Where is she, anyway?"

"We sent her to Iceland in your stead. Not happy about it, either," Connor said, as he grabbed his own breakfast, and followed the small group over to a table.

"Would anyone be? Better her than me, though." Ortega shuddered. "I hate the cold."

"Bjornson would be. He's the only nutter around here that loves it. Colder the better," Connor said, pulling a chair out for Ortega before she could put her breakfast on the table to do it herself.

Magnus grunted as she smiled at Connor again.

Ortega sat. Her gaze flicked up and down Magnus. "All that Viking blood, I bet."

Connor snorted. "You'd think. Bear blood. Polar Bear."

Ortega's dark brows arched, her expression changing to one of interest. "I've never met a polar bear shifter before."

Magnus' cheeks warmed. He couldn't say why.

"We all know you're a mind reader, and you know Raya is some kind of water spirit." Connor went on. "And I'm a white tiger. Now we all know everyone's secrets."

"Why, agent Ortega, I do believe you've made our Magnus blush." Burns' smooth voice turned mirthful.

"Too damned hot in here," Magnus grunted.

"Yeah, cuz it's not minus sixty-two in Ireland," Connor said. "But I believe you're right, Ms. Burns."

"Leaving in ten minutes," Magnus said, rising from the chair he'd barely occupied. "Don't be late."

"Fastest way to get on his bad side," Connor said to Ortega. "Stickler for punctuality.

"Oh, I know that already. I, uhm...was an hour late getting to the plane to come here."

"Huh, and you're here all in one piece. No chew marks or limbs missing." Connor's gaze flicked between Magnus and Ortega. "Ah, but then, you're cute."

Magnus stalked toward the door, growling, "Don't be late."

Burns' laughter followed him out.

FIVE

THEY RODE TO THE port in the same car she'd arrived in the day before.

Ana sat in the backseat with Raya. From her vantage point, she studied Bjornson's profile.

Pilot. Driver. Polar bear shifter.

Magnus had tied his long blond hair back in a French braid, exposing tattoos adorning the side of his neck below his hairline and behind his bearded jaw, disappearing below the collar of his leather jacket.

She couldn't see which vintage grunge band was on his t-shirt today.

What is that cologne he uses?

She blinked, turning her face away from her temporary teammate, toward the passenger window.

Focus, Ana. It doesn't matter what he smells like. He's your colleague and you have work to do. Do your job, crush the trafficking ring, and go back to your desk in California.

Her gaze drifted back. She couldn't recall the images that had flashed through her mind when they'd touched, when she'd been too distracted to close herself up.

Just the vision of whiteness before she'd passed out.

Her cheeks flamed.

I can't believe I passed out like that. Or the stupid things I said right before.

Awkward start. It was the fever.

She nodded to herself.

Yes, just an awkward start. Set it aside and don't be weird about it.

Resuming her gaze out the window, the port came into view.

Stacked containers hid the body of the ship, but the tower was unmistakable.

At one time, she'd been fascinated with ships of all kinds, because Antony had been a sailor and loved all things water-going.

Not anymore.

I hate this.

Her fingers flexed over her thighs as she rubbed her palms along the fabric of her pants.

Memories crashed through her.

Not mine.

Shared memories she gleaned from survivors and crew alike.

Prophetic images that warned her of Antony's accident.

Not the same.

She had to separate the situations from each other. One was work. The other was personal.

She squeezed her eyes shut. Drew a deep breath through her nose and eased it out between her lips.

Pressure on her forearm drew her attention.

Raya Burns' hand rested on Ana's sleeve, her expression one of compassion. She didn't say anything.

Raya knew.

She knew because she'd seen it, too.

Ana had seen it *all* first through Raya's memories.

Survivors trapped in shipping containers on the freighters. Barely fed or hydrated, dirty and cold, some sick. All headed for a life of enslavement to the highest bidders. Bidders that comprised human and paranormal buyers alike.

Anytime paranormals were involved, the GPSA was called in. And this team had been tracking this specific ring for some time before Ana had called Carson Perenga in to investigate a murder case that led them all together. Here.

She never could have imagined that the mutilated bodies that had turned up in her community on the west coast of California would bring them to this.

An international human trafficking ring, facilitated and organized by paranormals, which had led them to Raya Burns and her team.

The things she had seen in Raya's memories bit deep into Ana and still hadn't let go.

It changed her. Resolved her will to do all she could to help stop it.

Until Antony.

She'd changed, and she'd lost everything.

Ana forced a wan smile for Raya and whispered, "I'm good."

The look Raya gave her said *'bullshit'* but she maintained her silence and released Ana's arm.

Bjornson stopped the car outside the port office. The official on duty came out to meet them.

"Show time," Connor said, before stepping out of the car, Ana right behind him.

"Magnus, stay with Ana, no matter what. I'm going to look around while Connor entertains the officials," Burns said to Bjornson.

Even if Burns couldn't shift during the day, she still knew how to get around unseen. She knew how to be the ghost she became after nightfall.

A moment later, Ana sensed Bjornson at her back.

Used to working alone and taking care of herself, it surprised her that she found comfort in his presence as she turned her gaze toward the freighter looming above the port.

Sure, she'd worked with Carson, Lirikai, Raya, and Ian McLachlan on the last leg of the case, but that was different. Carson was like a big brother to her. Everyone else... sort of grew on her.

But this felt different.

The scent of Magnus' cologne mingled with the sea breeze encircling her.

Not now, Ana.

Focus.

She frowned at how easily she was becoming distracted by this man.

Not even Antony had distracted her in this way. At least, not until his death.

A surge of guilt warred with the sense of relief at realizing something other than the accident occupied her mind.

Neither were appropriate, at this time.

There was work to do.

Balance. Focus. Work.

The port official led them to another building on site, further away from the ship.

Ana eased the tension in her shoulders.

She'd board the ship later. People first.

As she trailed Connor and the official, she extracted her grandmother's crucifix and rosary from her jacket pocket. Looping the rosary around her wrist, she gripped the crucifix and beads in her palm, then checked her other pocket to ensure her phone hadn't slipped out.

Her thumb worried the smooth garnet beads as she sought balance, whispering her mantra with each breath.

Balance. Focus. Feel.

Her senses expanded around her, testing.

The general bustle of the place. The crisscross of natural and human energy.

The official's sadness. Connor's determination. Bjornson's concern.

She sucked in a breath as they stepped into the building.

She'd been expecting it, but it still took her breath away. Every time.

Inside, emotional energy corralled and turned over on itself. A heavy cloud.

It'll be worse on the ship.

They walked through an industrially decorated lobby, along a short corridor and through a double set of doors. Cots and chairs lined the large room where dozens of people slept, sat, or conversed. Medical personnel and local law enforcement were busy doing their jobs.

"They arrived in the wee hours. Near starved and filthy. Some are still getting cleaned up or having their first proper meal in weeks," the port official said.

Ana breathed through the suffocating storm cloud of collective heightened emotion. Her attention turned to a young woman curled up on a cot, staring at the empty one next to her.

Despair oozed from her.

Fear rippled toward Ana from a young man seated on the floor with his back pressed to the wall.

Anger rolled around the room as someone else raged at a police officer who was trying to take a statement.

Ana remembered to breathe. The ridges of the crucifix bit into the pad of her thumb.

Connor and the official were a dim memory as she moved around the room.

Bjornson, silent, moved two paces behind her.

Another young woman stood, leaning against the far wall, facing the room.

Numb.

Different.

She focused on this one.

Ana moved toward a table with a water carafe to fill a glass, then approached the young woman. Once she was in front of her, she realized the woman was much younger than she'd initially thought—a teen? Seventeen? Younger?

"Thirsty?" Ana held out the glass.

The girl turned her haunted gaze to Ana, lifted to Bjornson, then back to Ana and the glass. She shook her head.

Encouraged that the girl understood English, she pressed on.

"Can we talk?"

The girl shrugged.

"There's an empty office we can use," Bjornson murmured next to Ana's ear.

She turned to see the open door he indicated.

"There, okay?" Ana asked the girl.

Her gaze flicked toward the vacant room before she pushed away from the wall and preceded Ana toward it.

Still holding the glass of water, Ana straightened her shoulders and drew several steadying breaths as they followed.

You can do this, Ortega.

Set up for conducting business or interviews, the small room held a chair on one side and two on the opposite.

The girl dropped onto one of the two plastic chairs.

Ana set the glass on the table before her, then settled on the chair beside the girl, facing her.

Bjornson moved toward the back of the room, where he stood vigil.

"Do you mind if I record our chat? I'm an investigator."

Another shrug.

Ana extracted her phone from her pocket, found the voice app, turned it on, and set the device on the table. "I'm Analiese Ortega. What is your name?"

"Sascha," she mumbled, accent thick.

"Where are you from?"

"Varandey."

Ana repeated the answers for clarification on the recorder. "Have the authorities contacted your family yet?"

"No. I have none."

Ana studied Sascha's face. It was gaunt with a lack of basic needs. Her face and hands bore bruises, cuts, and scrapes. Ana suspected there'd be more under her clothes.

"You fought."

Sascha nodded. "I didn't want to get on another ship."

"Another ship," Ana repeated, thoughtful. "May I hold your hands?"

Sascha's gaze flicked to Ana's face, to her upturned palms with the crucifix and rosary and back to her face again. "I don't pray."

"No praying. Just talking."

"You are... a seer?"

"Something like that."

After another moment's hesitation, Sascha placed her frigid fingers over Ana's. Ana slid her hands forward, palms up under Sascha's. She drew another deep breath to allow the remnants of her mental barrier to fall away. She held Sascha's gaze as their energies fizzed.

Ana's hands felt as though they were frosting over, and she fought against a wave of fatigue.

Sascha's numbness was her own mental barrier, protecting her.

The emotion behind that barrier pressed upon them both, waiting for a fissure that Sascha wasn't ready to crack.

Yet.

Ana held firm, seeking.

Finally, after long moments, images flickered through.

But she wasn't seeing survivors like Sascha.

It was the familiar nightmare of Antony's naval vessel.

Ana released Sascha's hands, flexing her fingers.

Focus Ana. Focus!

She tried again.

This time, gaunt faces appeared as she searched Sascha's emotional memories of the last few weeks.

Despair. Fear. Rage.

Ana pressed deeper, seeking the faces of the perpetrators. Whispers of locations. Anything that could send them in the right direction.

Nothing.

Suddenly, the visions changed. Ana no longer guided the flow of memory and emotion. Sascha's numbness dissipated and everything else surged forward, stealing Ana's breath away.

She went rigid under the onslaught as Sascha's memory jerked back to the last beating at the hands of the guards. The last beating because a small group of men stopped it, fought back, protected her and the others in the dank room.

Their faces were familiar to Ana.

"Save them!" A disembodied voice shouted at her.

She flinched away from Sascha again, severing the energetic connection.

Balling her fists on her lap, she drew several deep breaths.

"Who were the men that protected you?"

"I don't know," Sascha said, trembling.

"The room wasn't on a ship."

"No. It was some kind of transfer place."

"Can you tell me more?"

Sascha shook her head as her body trembled.

Ana didn't want to push her too hard, but she wanted to know more about this transfer place.

"Can't you hear him?" Sascha said, eyes fixed behind Ana's left shoulder.

Ana glanced over her shoulder. She saw no one else.

"No. Who is there?"

"I don't know who he is. He just keeps screaming at you," she sobbed.

Save them.

Ana straightened. She'd heard it just once. She was so focused on Sascha, she didn't sense anyone else.

Still couldn't.

"Can you describe him?"

Sascha shook her head, squeezing her eyes shut. "No, I don't want to... dark hair... uniform of some kind. Same as the guys that protected me. Please, I don't want to talk anymore."

The numbness dissipated and emotion surged forward, overwhelming the space surrounding them.

Ana gasped as Sascha sobbed.

"Okay, Sascha, thank you. Thank you for talking to me," Ana said, voice soft as she struggled to reconcile the girl's emotions washing over her.

She closed her eyes, drew a deep, steadying breath, and when she opened them again, the chair across from her was empty.

As it had always been.

Elbows braced on her knees, she leaned forward until her forehead rested on her trembling hands.

"Are you all right?" Magnus' deep voice was quiet in the small room.

"Yes." She glanced at her phone on the table next to the untouched glass of water. She picked up the phone to speak into it. "Interview with bi-located victim in shock before she returned to her body." Ana's hands continued to tremble as she described the interviewee and what they said, since she couldn't be sure how much the recording would pick up of the conversation.

The phone slipped from her fingers, bouncing on the carpet.

Magnus scooped it up, sat across from Ana, and held it for her to finish her report.

When she finished, she turned the recorder off.

"Is it always like that?"

She shook her head. "You're pretty calm for someone that just watched me talk to an empty chair."

"It was a first." His lips quirked. "Who was the other person?"

"I-uhm... don't know." She swallowed.

Antony.

No, it couldn't be Antony. Wouldn't be Antony.

I can't sense anyone else.

"Probably another victim that didn't make it. But she mentioned a group of men trying to protect them in there. Uniforms. She mentioned *'some kind of uniforms'*."

Magnus nodded. "If you're good to continue, I'll contact Kane and find out if there are reports of missing servicemen, which doesn't fit the usual abductee profile."

"No, it doesn't. But yes, I'll move on to the other survivors. We have a long day ahead of us." She rubbed her palms down her thighs and gripped her knees.

Magnus placed a hand over one of hers. "Let me know how I can help."

Her gaze flicked up to his.

You can't.

"Thank you," she said, standing. "If I think of something, I will." She slipped her phone into her pocket and moved toward the door.

Drawing a breath, she straightened her shoulders and stepped back into the room of survivors to interview.

SIX

MAGNUS NEVER LEFT ANA'S side during the hours of interviews. He didn't think he could, even if he'd been ordered to.

No matter how pale she became or how much her hands trembled, she repeated the process again and again, recording each conversation.

There were no other eerie one-sided interviews like the first.

He'd been present when the tribal shamans conversed with the spirits.

This was different in as much that it lacked the ornate ceremony which normally accompanied the practice.

And yet, in her way, there had been similar points of respect. Permission, an offering, and an expression of gratitude.

Still, Magnus would admit to himself, if never anyone else, the experience had unsettled him. He preferred physical communication. Tangible. Anchored in *this* reality.

As he observed Agent Ortega throughout the day, the care and consideration which she approached every individual she spoke to never wavered.

In between sessions, she uploaded every recording to the cloud where any of the team members could access them. He knew Kane and Maeda would have them transcribed and reviewed within a few days. Neither cared to waste time or effort.

It wasn't until late evening, when the team packed up for the day, that a young woman approached agent Ortega.

"Sascha," Agent Ortega said.

The young woman nodded, hands wringing, gaze on the industrial carpet beneath their feet.

"How are you feeling?" Ortega asked, her voice soft.

"I—we... We spoke earlier?" Sascha asked, lifting her tear-swollen eyes to Ortega.

"We did."

This was the young woman Magnus couldn't see. What was it Ortega had said... bi-located? Not dead. Just... separated somehow. His heart twisted a little as he continued his role as observer.

"I don't understand. I thought it was a dream, but then, I've watched you talk to the others all day. And I don't think it was?"

"No, not a dream, but similar," Ana said, not elaborating.

Sascha seemed to accept this with a slight nod. "I've been thinking. Remembering. I don't want to, but I can't help it."

"It will take time, but you're safe now, Sascha."

Sascha blew out a breath, looking around the large room, and finally nodded.

"I know it here," she pointed to her head. "But here," she laid her hand over her sternum, "not so much."

Ortega gave her time to form what she wanted to say next. Magnus knew there was more. He could feel it himself, and he wasn't a psychic.

"Your recorder. Turn it on."

Ortega extracted it from her pocket and did as instructed.

"The man shouting at you, that you couldn't hear... had dark hair, as I said before, and a uniform of sorts—like the other men in the transfer station but blackened with dirt or smoke. He had a name tag that caught the light."

Magnus moved closer on hearing this.

Ortega didn't move, waiting.

"Ruiz. I think it read."

Ortega's whole body jerked, then went so still, Magnus doubted she drew a breath.

"Are you sure?" she finally asked, voice almost inaudible.

"Yes," Sascha nodded. "This I'm sure about."

"What else do you remember?"

"Just that he kept screaming '*save them, Ana, save them*'. It was very frightening."

Ortega remained quiet for a long moment.

"The men in the transfer station... did they have tags too?"

Sascha shook her head, swallowed hard, and dropped her gaze. "I'm sorry. I can't do this anymore. I had a friend... they took us at the same time. I don't know what happened to her." She lifted her gaze to Ana. Her eyes brimmed with tears.

"Of course, Sascha. When we find her, we will do what we can to reunite you. Thank you for talking to me. Earlier and now. And in the coming days, if you wish."

Sascha reached out to touch Ana's hand, as though testing her solidity. Ana squeezed her hand in return. "Eat some food and get rest. You did wonderfully today."

Sascha sniffled as Ortega released her hand, then threw her arms around Ana as she sobbed.

Ortega embraced the young woman and let her cry as long as she needed. Magnus stood at Ortega's back, observing it all, chest tight.

Everything they heard, every piece of data they collected today, would be added to all the rest of the data they'd collected over the years since they started investigating these traffickers.

We're so close. So, damned, close.

Gods, I want to shut these fuckers down and make them pay for what they've done to so many innocent people.

So many victims stolen. Families fractured, communities mourning.

And for what?

So someone can make money.

He swallowed his revulsion and calmed the rush of emotion before approaching Ortega and the survivor, Sascha.

Sascha let go of Ortega and moved away without another word.

He glanced up at movement across the room. Connor and Burns waited by the door.

"Time to go," he whispered by Ortega's shoulder.

She turned to look up at him, eyes haunted, as she acknowledged his words with a nod.

In that instance, he wanted nothing more than to pull her into his arms and give her the comfort she'd given so many others this day.

Instead, he followed her out of the room to join the others who'd moved out into the hall. They both studied Ortega with grim expressions. Burns rubbed Ortega's shoulder, but said nothing.

They walked back to the car and Magnus drove them back to Kane's estate.

Each team member was silent as they reflected on their day's work, mentally preparing for the next.

"YOU'RE TELLING ME WE lost another fucking ship?" Adolf Wulker's heart pounded as he stared at his subordinate.

"Yes, sir, but we used our connections to put up some jurisdictional roadblocks. They shouldn't be able to trace the ship's point of origin."

"But another ship, with all of its cargo, is lost. That shipment had a very particular order for a very important client." Wulker's fist slammed the top of his solid oak desk, making loose objects jump and rattle.

"How did we lose it in the first place?" He held up a hand, stopping the other man from speaking. "No. Never mind, I don't care. This careless loss of merchandise is going to stop. Now. See to it."

The assistant dry-swallowed and croaked. "Yes, sir."

Wulker waved him away.

"An unfortunate by-product of any trade business. A reasonable insurance write-off." The forgotten blonde woman in the corner of the room said, as she rose to her feet.

Recalling her presence, Wulker scowled at her. "This one was lost in *your* territory."

She breezed toward him. "My brother was aboard that ship, but I trust he'll have evacuated with the crew, yes?"

He couldn't help himself. Despite his annoyance, desire surged through him as his gaze swept her pouty lips, full breasts, narrow waist, and generous hips.

Adolf nodded.

"I'll talk to my people," she murmured, pressing her soft breasts to his chest.

Unable to resist, his hand drifted down her waist to her ass and groped as she leaned in to kiss him. As his arousal grew, his hand shifted, splitting into two distinct tentacles extending from his cuff, drifting lower down her hip. One encircled her thigh, the other drifted up under the hem of her short skirt, teasing.

She moaned.

He grinned, enjoying the power he had over her.

He stepped back, releasing her. His limbs merged, returning to human form. "Set up a meeting. We need to discuss a change in procedure."

She frowned at the extra space he put between them. "Of course."

"Impress the importance that this meeting be face to face."

"My former father-in-law won't be eager for that, no matter that we've... persuaded him otherwise."

"I'm well aware of how difficult he is to control, despite the formidable power of my venom's persuasion. I'm also aware he doesn't welcome outsiders to clan territory, nor does he like to leave his people for any length of time. As you've reminded me. But if he wishes to continue to provide them with security and prosperity, then he will meet with me."

"Where and when shall I propose this meeting take place?"

"I'll keep it simple. The stronghold. As soon as possible."

She arched her brow, nodded, and left the room.

"An unfortunate by-product indeed," he murmured as he approached the vast window of his office overlooking the skyline of Barentia across the narrow channel.

Maybe once the meeting details were set, he would accept her less-than-subtle offer of intimate play time.

For now, there was work to do.

Work first, play later.

However, Adolf did allow himself to indulge in just a few moments of fantasizing about their future bedroom escapades. He did prefer to plan *everything*, after all.

SEVEN

ANA'S BREATH SHUDDERED AS she popped her earpiece in place before embarking on the freighter.

She moved aboard the ship, both hands grasping her phone, carefully positioned close to her midsection so she wouldn't accidentally touch anything.

That would come later.

Magnus, her ever-present shadow, moved silently several paces behind.

She still found it difficult to grasp just how such a large man could move with such stealth.

Equally, while she couldn't comprehend her instinctual acceptance of his nearness consciously, she willfully accepted it.

Regardless of her comfort level, her fingers still drifted over the reassuring presence of her taser tucked safely away should she need it. The ship had been checked, but it was always a possibility that someone could hide if they knew the nooks and crannies well enough.

She glanced over her shoulder.

Magnus' gaze swept the deck of the ship, assessing. Fierce, determined concentration.

Anyone looking to tangle with that man was on a mission of serious self-harm, or had lost their reason.

Forcing her attention back to the task at hand, she switched on her recorder and began her own method of investigation.

Balance. Focus. Feel.

Speaking in a voice low enough for the earpiece to pick up her voice, yet quiet enough that most humans couldn't pick out the words, she made her way across and through the ship, documenting everything she observed.

Physically and psychically.

She welcomed the familiar haze.

Aware of her surroundings yet lost in the mental images and sensations bombarding her, she struggled at first to just let them flow around and through her.

Her breath came fast under the onslaught. Every muscle in her body fought against it, tense and rigid. Until she repeatedly reminded herself to surrender.

At the top of the metal stairs leading down into the hold, she hesitated.

Revulsion rippled through her.

That self-preservative part of her was screaming not to descend.

That way led to too much pain.

What sane person would willfully inflict the torrential pain of others on themselves?

Her breath hitched.

But isn't that why Antony left you in the first place?

Because you no longer operated like a sane person?

He died believing that.

"Agent Ortega? Are you alright?" Magnus' voice was muffled in her current state.

Magnus.

"Ana?" His voice broke the spell.

She blinked. "Yes, I'm fine."

She descended the stairs. It was several degrees colder below deck and growing colder the deeper she went.

The temperature change was both natural and supernatural.

"A few of the victims died down here," she murmured, moving ever closer to the holding crate.

The GPSA team hadn't found any digital trackers, documents, or maps left behind. The crew must have disposed of them into the ocean or taken them with them when they escaped.

Otherwise abandoned, the ship had drifted with its cargo.

It was that information that they needed.

The departure point and destination point.

Balance. Focus. Feel.

First, she had to document what she could register below decks.

She drew another deep breath and allowed her instinct to guide her. Moving along one corridor, she followed it until it opened up to the main hold and kept going until she stood before the steel containers.

In her mind's eye, she could see all of them, victims and crewmen alike, in various states, dependent on what their strongest emotions were at the time they were in this place.

A suffocating jumble. Still, she opened herself up as wide as possible, flowing through it all until *something* tugged at her.

The energetic signature of shifters, not the signatures of the human cargo.

Focusing on those, she moved toward another area where rusty splotches stained the floor.

Pain.

She tensed as her protective barrier slammed into place, blocking everything out.

"Dammit!"

I need better control.

She drew a breath. Held it and tried again.

But all she could sense now, was the distinct polar bear shifter signature that she identified with Magnus now that she knew what he was.

"I need more space. Wait here," she said, and moved away from him, crossing the stained floor to the other wall.

But it didn't make any sense. The signature was stronger here, where it should have been weaker when she moved away from Magnus.

Save them.

Antony.

Ana froze, swallowing a sob of frustration.

How can I do my job if my guilt over Antony's accident keeps interfering?

She straightened her shoulders, determined to ignore the echo of Antony's voice from her nightmares.

Moving further away from Magnus, she tried to grasp the faint tethers of energy that had drawn her here to begin with.

Still rife with polar bear shifter energy, she followed it anyway. Maybe it wasn't Magnus she was picking up on after all, since it led away from him.

Curious, she followed the energy trail. Which led her to another section of the ship.

A vast room containing the ship's engine, with pipes and machinery jutting out of it in what seemed like controlled chaos to Ana.

The signature that guided her here lost its direction and seemed to surround her now. Unable to pinpoint where to go next, she resigned herself to placing a hand on the steel railing between herself and the engine.

But not just yet.

Realizing she'd forgotten to talk through her path, she quickly recapped where she was.

"Energy signature similar to Agent Bjornson's led me to the engine room from the cargo hold. I'm going to make first physical contact here." She finally placed her hand on the rail and continued to move forward as she searched through the images of crewmen that had been here until she found the person associated with the signature.

The vision of a young man, similar in build to Bjornson, crouched along this rail, injured.

She followed it to the end, where a bank of steel paneled controls faced her.

Save them.

An overpowering sense of urgency surged through her. She dropped her phone into her pocket and placed both hands on the massive control box. Moving around the side of the control panels, she saw a gap between it and the wall, close to floor level.

The urgency increased, and she found a section with a missing panel.

"Here," she shouted to Bjornson as she got down on her hands and knees. "There's something here."

Unable to see into the darkness of the cramped space, she reached out a hand, seeking whatever hid in the box.

She hadn't expected her hand to land on what felt like a foot. A cold human foot.

Startled, she cried out and fell back.

Bjornson appeared beside her. "Are you alright?"

"There's someone in there. I don't know if they're alive or not."

He left her to peer into the space, pulling out his phone to aim its light into the darkness.

"Shit. We've got a body hidden inside the engine room's control panels," he spoke into his earpiece. "Vital status un-determined."

As soon as the shock of finding a human body rather than an object passed, Ana approached and replaced her hand on the foot, trying to sense their spirit. "I think they're still alive. Yes! He's alive, but barely."

Within minutes, an emergency response team arrived and got to work extracting the survivor.

Now they just had to determine who this man—polar bear shifter—was, and why he was there.

MAGNUS ANXIOUSLY STOOD ASIDE while the medical team worked to free the man hidden inside the engine room's control panel.

"Magnus, he's a shifter." Ana's voice was quiet.

He looked down into her upturned face, tight with concern. "A polar bear shifter, like you."

The blood drained from his face. If that were the case, why hadn't he recognized the scent right away? And what the hell was one of his kind doing aboard this ship? Who was he?

Magnus crouched next to the opening again while the crew worked to remove the steel framing of the box surrounding the pipes and wires to determine how to extract the man safely.

He inhaled, scenting.

Yes, now he could pick out the distinct, faint scent familiar to him, but it wasn't right. Familiar yet distorted. It was... other. Someone he knew. Polar bear, yes, but tainted.

Finally, after cutting through the steel paneling, the team lifted it off, allowing the light to wash over the hidden man.

The side panel came away, and the man rolled free, unconscious.

"Fuck." Magnus barked, chest tight, as he shoved team members aside to get a closer look at the man's face. "Aksel Matochkin."

As gently as he could, he lifted him off the floor and carried him to the awaiting gurney so the medics could work on him right away.

He backed off to give them space, listening as they assessed.

"We need to get him to GPSA Medics," he said to Ana.

She nodded and pulled her phone from her pocket to make the call.

By the time the medical team could safely bring their patient out of the ship and transferred to the docks, the GPSA medical staff were already landing via a nearby helipad to take him into custody.

Magnus helped load Aksel into the helicopter, identifying him as one of his clansmen.

His instinct was to accompany him to see to his care and find out how the hell he was on this ship.

But that would have to wait. Answers would have to wait. For now, Magnus had to trust the GPSA medical team to do their jobs while he did his.

He and Ana still had work to do aboard the ship.

EIGHT

ANA RUBBED HER FINGERS across the back of her neck, kneading the muscles as she listened to the rest of her teammates give their reports to Kane, now that they were all back at the estate.

After the extraction of Magnus' clansman, Ana had continued her investigation with little success. The only directional intention she could glean was 'north', which was pretty darned useless as far as she was concerned.

She looked up as Magnus crossed the back of the room again.

He was with them in body, but his mind was visibly with his clansman.

"Bjornson, will you sit? Your pacing is making me twitchy," Aaron Connor snapped, cutting into what Raya was saying.

Magnus scowled at Aaron, but dropped into the leather chair next to Ana.

Raya resumed.

Ana tuned out Raya's words as Magnus' energy swarmed her, stealing her breath away.

"I'm sure he'll be alright. Our medics are the best." She reached out, hesitated for only a second to ensure her psychic barrier was in place, then laid her hand over his on the arm of the chair.

Magnus blew out his breath, looking down at her hand on his. "I know. He flipped his hand over, so they were palm to palm, giving her fingers a slight squeeze.

Shivers rippled through her at the intimate contact. She struggled against the urge to slide her fingers between his, anchoring them together.

She looked up into his face, his eyes locked on hers, thoughtful.

"He would have died in there if you hadn't found him."

"Maybe, maybe not," she said, trying to make light of her role.

Magnus snorted. "He's a polar bear. If he's unconscious, he's in a bad way." He glanced at the door.

"Magnus, what else can you tell us about our patient?" Director Kane asked, drawing the focus of the meeting back to Bjornson.

Palm still tingling, Ana withdrew her hand from Magnus' light grasp.

"There really isn't anything more I can add to the report I filled out earlier."

Kane picked up the sheaf of paper. "Aksel Matochkin, twenty-two years old, kinsman by marriage via your former wife, Ulla Matochkin."

Magnus nodded.

Former wife?

Magnus was—had been married? Ana wasn't sure why it surprised her, given that she knew nothing about the man next to her. It had only been a few days since she boarded his charter.

"When's the last time you saw Aksel?"

Magnus drew a deep breath and blew it out on a heavy exhale, staring at the floor. "The day they banished me."

Banished?

Ana's gaze shot to Magnus' solemn face, then to Kane and the others.

They all know.

Despite not being a shifter, even Ana knew that banishment from a clan was bad.

Very bad.

And he worked for Kane and the GPSA? How the heck did that make sense? What could he possibly have done that was so bad, that the only answer was banishment? Or death.

She glanced at him again and decided she was glad it was the former.

But if he worked for Kane, it couldn't be *so* bad, could it?

She'd never got that kind of vibe from him, not even when she'd accidentally read him on that first night. Which knocked her out. Along with the fever. She still blamed *that* mostly on the fever.

Or... had it been something more?

She searched his profile, tempted to lower her barrier and prod. But that would be an invasion of his privacy.

Not something she would deliberately do to her teammates unless directly ordered to do.

Deliberate reading or not, she couldn't ignore the waves of guilt and regret that emanated from him. And something more. Deeper. Heartache.

The urge to take his hand and offer him comfort again was overwhelming.

Heartache for his former wife?

She clasped her hands on her lap, fingers locked together as she passingly acknowledged her own fleeting feelings of disappointment and jealousy.

Jealousy?

You've barely known the man a few days, she reminded herself. *What's wrong with you?*

She entertained the notion for a few seconds. Only a few. That was all she needed.

Tall, amazing hair, muscle-y in that bear-like way and smells really, really great.

Then she promptly shut that line of thought down.

Colleague. Grumpy—in a cute way. Colleague. Professional. Gentleman. Colleague.

She recalled waking in her burrito-blanket-roll, eyes opening to the image of his bare-chested form sleeping upright on an office chair.

Who does that?

That doesn't sound much like the type of guy that gets himself banished from his clan, does it?

Ana!

She squeezed her eyes shut to control her wayward thoughts.

She was so busy self-analyzing that she missed when the topic changed.

"... when he wakes up. Otherwise, you'll have to investigate this further," Kane said.

"You mean go home and talk to my father?" Magnus spat the words. "You know, I might not make it that far if they have orders to kill me as soon as I cross the territorial boundary."

"They won't, and you know it."

"No, they'd want to know why I was there first, then kill me."

"So, you give them a reason that would get you in to see him."

"Death or marriage."

Kane raised a brow. "Explain."

"Normally when someone is banished, that's it. They're dead to the clan. However, as the king's heir and son, proof of death would be necessary, therefore my body would need to be returned."

"And marriage?"

"Along the same lines as death. The registrar needs to record vital information in the clan histories. They must keep the information tracking the lineages. If I were to marry, this would logically lead to an heir that could return and challenge for leadership at some point, despite *my* position of banishment."

King's heir and son? Magnus was a polar bear prince?

Ana was dying to know why they banished Magnus from his clan.

"Okay, that's perfect. If we can't rouse your brother-in-law to consciousness in the next day or two, you're going to your father to report your marriage."

"What?" Magnus shot to his feet.

"Well, you can't go and report your death now, can you? Marriage it is."

He snorted, throwing his hands up. "And who am I supposed to present to him as my wife?"

Kane seemed thoughtful as she regarded him. "Not Burns. They'd smell her and know instantly she isn't human, which would raise suspicions. That leaves Ortega."

"What—what?" Ana popped to her feet next to Magnus. "I can't marry Bjornson!"

"Hey, no one said anything about actually getting married," Magnus growled. "Besides, Ortega's too frail to even survive the trip there."

"I'm not frail!" she objected, fists landing on her hips.

"Sweetheart, anyone who gets hypothermia from a rainstorm is frail," Magnus rounded on her, brows furrowed.

"Well... I..." She crossed her arms. "Whatever, I don't want to go anyway, so it's a moot point."

"Want to or not. Your orders are to go to Barentia and pretend to be Magnus' bride-to-be if his kinsman doesn't wake up to explain what the hell he was doing on that ship."

"Bride-to-be..." Magnus grumbled as he sat next to Aksel's hospital bed, which had been set up in a room at Kane's estate. GPSA medics that knew how to handle shifter physiology closely monitored him.

Despite the ridiculous proposal, the underlying seriousness of Aksel's state was undeniable. He was alive—barely, but he wasn't healing either.

Magnus studied the younger man's bruised face. He'd been carefully cleaned up, his broken leg encased in a cast. The grime had obscured many cuts and bruises, testament to the fact he'd been beaten—severely. Many times.

Magnus swallowed hard. Aksel was still a kid the last time they'd seen each other, and it hadn't been a happy parting.

Obviously. There was nothing happy about a banishment where everyone was expected to treat the banished like a pariah as they cast him out, hurling objects and bitter words.

Before that day, Aksel had been like Magnus' own little brother. He'd certainly loved him like he was his blood.

Blood didn't matter anymore. Nor did kinship. None of those things existed in Magnus' world since he'd been cast out.

I can't go back.

His father had ensured that.

He rubbed a hand over his face and beard, scrubbing the memories away as he moved to sit in the chair at the foot of Aksel's bed.

Why the fuck was Aksel on that ship? He wasn't human—he was a powerful member of Barentia's polar bear shifter clan. So how is it possible for him to even be in this state? Prone, vulnerable and near death, unable to heal, let alone awaken and tell Magnus what happened to him.

Even when Magnus had experienced the worst of the worst in clan life by being banished, no matter what they'd thrown at him, or insults they'd hurled, he'd still had his physical strength to keep him alive, alone in the frozen northern wastelands.

When he'd almost died of starvation, or drowning from swimming for days, exhausted, he'd still healed.

Aksel wasn't healing.

Why?

Magnus' gaze swept over Aksel's prone form. The blanket covered most of his body, leaving his clan markings visible above it. A mixture of his Matochkin home clan and Barentian adoptive clan.

Magnus swallowed down the long-buried homesickness that threatened to rise. He hadn't seen such familiar body art, other than his own, in a decade.

As he looked at the young man's exposed tattoos, Magnus noticed one that stood out, stark and fresh on the base of his throat, but partially obscured by his thick beard.

Magnus rose from his chair and approached the bed, bending to inspect Aksel's throat.

His stomach dropped, his heart stopped, and he closed his eyes.

Fuck.

Leaning on the rail at the foot of the bed, he forced himself upright.

He gave himself a moment to collect his despair and his rage before reaching for his phone to call Kane.

"We've got a problem. A big one."

NINE

ANA GLANCED AT THE text that flashed across her phone, which lay on her bed while she dried her hair and sighed.

'Meet in my office asap.'

She'd only had enough time to shower after the long, long day and what seemed to be an even longer meeting.

I can't believe Kane even suggested I pretend to be engaged to Magnus. What a ridiculous ruse.

And yet, nothing about Kane's demeanor hinted at any type of humor.

She glanced at the phone again.

Kane wouldn't call them back to her office if it weren't important.

Ana scrubbed her hair as quickly as she could with the towel that encircled her head, then threw on her silk nightgown and reached for her robe. Shoving her bare feet into her fuzzy slippers, she belted her robe and left her room as Raya was leaving hers, still fully dressed, her brows deeply furrowed with concern.

She gave Ana a cursory once over and smirked. "Cute slippers."

"Any idea what this is about?"

Raya shrugged. Her concerned expression returned, "Nope, but we should hurry."

At that, they jogged the rest of the way.

They arrived at Kane's open office door, where she was still at her desk. Connor sat in the leather chair that Ana had occupied earlier in the evening while Magnus stood by Kane's desk with a haunted expression.

Ana's stomach churned.

What could have happened in the last twenty minutes that was so urgent?

Aksel Matochkin was stable and in the care of GPSA medics. Had he taken a turn?

Kane gestured for them to sit.

"What's happened?" Raya said as she took the other chair.

Ana perched on the same antique chair from the first day, arms crossed.

"Aksel is marked."

"Shit," Connor spat.

"Oh no," Raya whispered, turning wide eyes on Magnus. "Oh no."

"Marked? What do you mean?" Ana demanded after seeing their reactions.

"Magnus, would you show Ana the picture?" Kane said.

Magnus withdrew his phone and swiped his screen, producing an image.

Ana rose from her seat and approached to see a human throat with a black ink sigil at its base.

"A tattoo? On his throat?" She looked up at Magnus, who nodded. "What does it mean?"

"It seems to be some kind of hex," Raya said, her voice full of disgust.

"Magic?" Ana said, incredulous. "But... why?"

"It's most likely the reason he isn't healing. It's keeping him weak."

"And unconscious?"

"Not by design. He's unconscious because he was beaten so badly and cannot heal naturally because of the sigil. Medical science is doing its best to support his body where his shifter ability can't."

"But I still don't know what this sigil means. Why would he have it? Is it something to do with the trafficking ring?"

"Yes," Kane said. "It's the mark of one of the sector heads that we're tracking. We've only seen it a few times, and it's never resulted in anything good."

"What do you mean?" Ana's hand shot to her chest, fingers tugging on the edges of her robe as her anxiety spiked.

Dark magic is way out of my league.

"It means that unless we can find a way—which we haven't yet—to break this hex, the only way we can communicate with Aksel is through you."

All the blood drained from Ana's face and a chill swept through her like a north front.

"I—I see." She drew a breath. "And what if I can't?"

"Then we're going into clan territory completely blind," Magnus said.

"LIKE HELL I'M GOING into polar bear clan territory!" Ana squeaked at Kane, eyes wide, still gripping the front of her thin robe across her throat. She freed a hand to swipe the air in front of her. "N—No. I agreed to Iceland, for Carson—who's not even frigging here, by the way! But the Barents Sea? No.

No way." She turned toward Magnus, jabbing the air in his direction with a pointed finger. "No."

Then she spun around in her fuzzy slippers and stomped out of the Director's office, the bottom edges of her robe billowing out behind her.

Burns stared after Ana, mouth gaping. "I've never seen her lose her shit like that before. She's always so damned calm, like an unruffled cat."

"Seems that cat just got her tail stomped on. Good job, Magnus. Great way to break the new recruit in."

"Shut up, Connor," Magnus growled as he followed Ana out—and not sure why he did.

Just to calm her down and make her see reason, he told himself, since Kane had insisted that she was the only agent that could do this mission.

Which he seriously, seriously doubted.

There has to be someone else that can do it. Someone that won't shrivel at the sight of snow.

Still, Magnus didn't like to see her so rattled. Especially not after how she'd handled herself for the last couple of days. She'd been so empathetically solid for all of those survivors they'd interviewed. So calm and collected as she led their team through the ship to find his near-dead clansman.

And she hadn't even been working on these cases nearly as long as he and the others had.

Just before he caught up to her billowing robes, halfway down the hall to their rooms, he admitted to himself he respected her.

Her professionalism and compassion in the face of such hardship.

"Ana."

"No." Her index finger jabbed the air as she swung her arm out behind her, but she didn't slow her pace.

Two more strides and Magnus reached for her arm, trying to slow her without hurting her. "Listen."

"I. Am not—." She heaved a deep breath. "Going. To The *North*. I'm not." She shook her head, eyes wild as she looked at him, then up and down the hall in case anyone else was coming to force her into the barren frozen wilderness. "Not happening."

"If you would just listen—."

"Nope. Nuh-uh. As I said, I was willing to go to Iceland for Carson because he's like a brother and he's always had my back. Thank *God*, I ended up here instead. And now, what? You're going to try to make me go into hostile territory? I'm not trained for that. It's so much worse than Iceland." She sobbed on the last few words.

"You're exhausted."

"You're demented," she snapped.

"And you're being rude again." Noting the red splotches of color appearing on her cheeks. Just like it did before she passed out in the hangar. He tried to take a softer approach. "Ana, you've pushed yourself really hard these last few days. Get some rest and we can talk about this tomorrow."

She'd handled herself impeccably, and now, at the mention of going to his homeland, she was losing her shit? It was the Iceland incident all over again.

"Magnus, I can't."

Something about those three words and the haunted look in her eyes cracked his heart. Her lower lip trembled.

"I told Carson I wasn't ready. Maeda knows it. This is way over my head."

Magnus reached for Ana, wrapping his arms around her trembling body, trying to comfort her.

She sagged against him. "If I couldn't save Antony, how can I save anyone else? And now there's black magic involved?"

Magnus didn't answer. He didn't have one to give, so he just held her. After a moment, her hands slid around his waist, and she held him back.

Closing his eyes, he rested his cheek on the top of her damp hair, inhaling the fragrance of her.

Coconut and vanilla and Ana.

The way she fit in his arms...the way hers felt around him...felt... *Right*.

He smiled against the top of her head when he felt her thumb stroking his spine.

Ana turned her face, resting her forehead against his chest, and drew a deep breath.

"You always smell so good," she murmured.

"So do you." He lifted his head from hers, inhaling her scent again.

Memorizing it, as though he hadn't already.

She leaned back just enough to look up into his face. Her eyes shimmered in the low light of the hallway they still stood in.

He wished they were in his room, or hers.

She searched his face.

What is she looking for?

His gaze dropped to her plump lips, waiting for her to say what she was thinking, or ask a question.

He hadn't expected her little pink tongue to dart out, to moisten her lips.

That tiny movement undid Magnus. A growl rumbled through his chest.

Her fingers clutched at his back now as her face tilted up to his descending lips.

Her mouth was ripe and lush, warm and inviting as the entire length of her body pressed to his.

He was suddenly hyper-aware that the only barrier between them was her thin nightgown and robe.

Dear gods, he wanted to take her to bed.

He hardened against the warmth of her belly, and she pressed into him even more.

Her tongue swept his lower lip, drawing him in.

He growled a second time, forcing her back a step to pin her body between his and the ornate wallpaper.

She gasped against his lips as his thigh moved between hers, pressing into her heat, eliciting a moan.

"Magnus," she gasped.

His name, like that, from her... too much.

His hands moved up to her shoulders, caressing their way up her collar bones to her delicate throat to cradle her face as he kissed her.

His voice was low, almost a whisper of restraint as he spoke, a breath away from her soft lips.

"Ana, sweetheart, if you don't want to finish this," he paused, drawing a breath, "then we should part ways here."

Her sweet breath shuddered against his, her body pliant, her lips parted.

All he had to do was lift the hem of her gown and she'd be his. It was all he had in him to resist the temptation to slide his palm along her thigh, to draw it up around his hip and settle into her heat.

She didn't move as she considered his words.

His heart pounded in time with his throbbing cock.

He drew a deep breath to clear the lightheadedness, but all it did was embed the scent of the woman locked in indecision before him.

Slowly, she dropped her forehead to his chest as she slid her palms around from his back to his abdomen before she leaned back against the wall.

Releasing her face, Magnus' hands retraced their path back down to her shoulders. He slid them along the length of her arms till he found her hands.

Taking them in his, giving them a little squeeze before releasing her, he backed a step, pulling her with him as they continued down the hall, the fingers of his right hand still entwined with those of her left until they found her room.

At her door, he lifted her fingertips and brushed his lips across her knuckles before letting go of that last little bit of contact and regaining full control over his body.

She reached for the doorknob, then turned to look at him, about to say something.

His heartbeat quickened.

She settled on, "Good night, Magnus."

He nodded, "Good night, Ana." He turned, striding toward his room. He heard her door click shut just before he reached his.

TEN

ANA DRAGGED HERSELF OUT of bed, stumbled toward the shower, and forced her chaotic, exhausted emotions into a semblance of order.

After a kiss like that, how could anyone sleep?

Every inch of her body was hypersensitive and wound to the point of snapping.

All she could think about was the taste, smell, and feel of Magnus.

Magnus! How the heck had that happened?

She turned on the shower faucet with a snap.

It had all seemed to happen so quickly and without warning.

A moment of comfort quickly turned into something more.

When had she decided she wanted him before her brain knew it?

A small inner voice told her. She knew exactly when.

She tested the water before disrobing and stepped under the stream of warm water.

That first night on the tarmac when he'd taken her hand and helped her board the plane after lifting her suitcases like paper bags.

She soaped her loofah.

The sensation of being enveloped in his arms... heaven. She'd never, ever, felt so secure as she had in that moment.

Like the world outside of their little impulsive sphere didn't matter.

God, that kiss—had almost made her feral.

The memory of his growl, low and deep, reverberating through her, igniting every erogenous zone in her body.

She slid her soapy hands over her skin, reveling in the cascade of warm water, imagining Magnus' lips following the trail of water over her taut nipples.

This wasn't helping to calm her nerves.

Her fingers found her core, gasping as they brushed over her sensitive, throbbing nub.

She needed the release that hadn't found its natural end last night. It had only grown. Her fingers worked to find it.

Magnus.

The gentle rasp of his silky beard against her skin, his soft lips and the sweep of his tongue on hers.

She gasped and moaned, pulsing around her fingers, body finally sagging under the cleansing water.

She drew a deep, shuddering breath, opened her eyes and stared at the tiles until they focused again and finished her shower.

There was work to do, and she couldn't afford to be distracted.

MAGNUS STOOD NEXT TO Aksel's inert body. The medical equipment monitoring his vitals assured him he was still alive.

Kane stood by the window, glaring at her phone, furiously tending to emails while they waited.

Magnus glanced at his watch and, like magic, Ana appeared in the open doorway.

She paused, gave him a curt nod, and glanced in Kane's direction, who waved in acknowledgment, then approached the bed.

With Aksel's bed between them, Magnus assessed Ana's expression.

She focused on Aksel, her demeanor serious and professional.

As though last night had never happened.

Neither said anything until Kane approached, dropping her phone into her jacket pocket. "Are you ready?" she asked Ana.

"There's never any guarantee with this," she warned.

"I know. I'm also aware that you've already given a lot over the last few days. But we need this."

Ana's gaze swept Magnus' face before turning back to Aksel.

"Okay." She pulled her phone from her pocket, set it to record, and drew a deep breath. "What do you want me to focus on?"

"The sigil," Kane said.

"How he ended up on that ship." Magnus answered at the same time without looking at Kane.

"They're probably connected, right?" she murmured as she turned her focus away from the other occupants of the room and trained her energy on Aksel, then opened her senses.

For a long time, she stood beside the man, seeking to connect with his energy.

"His signature is still weak. All I can detect from him is that he vibrates on the same level as Magnus. That's how I knew he was a shifter, and what kind." She frowned. "He didn't draw me to him. It must have been something else that led me to find him. He's not reaching out—like he's locked inside."

"The sigil," Kane repeated.

Ana set the phone on a level spot on the mattress and extracted her Gran's garnet rosary from her pocket. She wrapped the beads around her left wrist and gripped the crucifix between her thumb and forefinger.

Ana held her right hand over Aksel's bare forearm and planted her feet.

Balance. Focus. Feel.

Her fingers hovered over the fine red hairs of his freckled arm a moment before descending the last few inches to rest on his cool flesh.

A wave of frigid water washed over her, stealing her breath away, followed by flashes of a white barren landscape, the face of a beautiful blond woman, and then the sensation of fists connecting with flesh and bone before the pain of impact on her face, and gut.

It all hit her in a matter of seconds, leaving her gasping and doubled over.

"Ana!" Magnus' voice pulled her from the haze of pain and suffocation.

Her hand snapped open, releasing Aksel's arm.

She dragged a hard, gasping breath into her lungs. "I'm okay," she croaked, struggling for more air before describing what she saw.

Her gaze flicked over Aksel's still inert form, curling her right hand into a tight fist. "It doesn't mean anything. You can guess all of that just by looking at him."

"Try again."

"Kane, just give her a minute. She's already exhausted from the last few days," Magnus growled.

Kane turned to him, brow raised. "I am well aware, Agent Bjornson." To Ana, she said, "Agent Ortega, when you're ready to resume your work, place your palm over the sigil."

Ana warily looked from Magnus to Kane to Aksel's pale, bruised face.

Maeda had warned her against direct contact with such things during their training sessions.

After that first reading, she wasn't sure she was ready to touch the sigil. It could do anything to her.

Lifting her left hand, she pressed her lips to Gran's silver crucifix, whispering a prayer as she repositioned her stance next to the bed.

She ignored Magnus and Kane, focusing all her attention on Aksel's face.

This was about *him*. A victim, like all the others, she hoped to God would be a survivor, unlike so many of those they couldn't reach.

Flexing the fingers of her right hand, she pressed her palm to the black ink sigil at the base of Aksel's throat and closed her fingers in a firm grasp.

This time, it was a wave of suffocating black ink that washed over her, rather than frigid water, forcing her to her knees.

Still, she didn't let go.

Her grip on Aksel was her lifeline to reality.

She couldn't let go.

ELEVEN

MAGNUS LUNGED FORWARD, DESPERATE to separate Ana from his kinsman.

"No!" Kane slipped between Ana and him and shoved him back with such unexpected force that his back hit the wall several feet behind him. "Let her do her job."

Magnus was startled by a glow in Kane's eyes he'd never seen before as her voice pinned him in place.

Then he realized she hadn't physically touched him.

What the fuck?

He snarled at her. "Release me."

"Not until you understand you cannot interfere."

He struggled against the invisible bond.

"I know this is harming her and what the risks are, Magnus. We have no choice. She is meant to do this, as are you."

"What the fuck does that mean?" He couldn't unpin his spine from the wall or force his arms forward more than an inch or two.

"It doesn't matter. We need all the information she can get about this sigil, Magnus."

The raw emotion in her voice took some of the fight out of him.

"Burns and Connor left this morning to meet with Lirikai, Perenga and McLachlan in Iceland. They're getting closer to the location of the hub. But this sigil changes everything. We have to know more before we move in."

His gaze fixed on Ana's kneeling, trembling form. He stopped struggling against Kane.

She released him without another word or movement.

He scrubbed a hand over his face and back through his hair. "We've seen it a few times before. Why the concern now?"

"As agents, you're not kept up to date on all the survivors' post-rescue. You go on to the next job, and the next." She turned her gaze to Aksel. "Every one of them is still in a disconnected state. That sigil is the only difference between those victims and the ones that we've recovered that have healed and are trying to move on with their lives."

"So, Aksel might remain like this?"

"Yes. Maybe? We—I don't know."

"And how will this affect Ana?" He swallowed the lump rising in his throat.

"I don't know that either," Kane said, voice raw.

When she returned his direct gaze, her expression was full of concern, regret and resolve.

There was nothing he or she could do.

It was up to Ana.

ANA AWAKENED IN A black filmy undertow.

Pulled and pushed in all directions, unable to draw breath.

Trapped. Weak. Disconnected.

Prey to the whispers.

Something tapped against her palm. Her hand closed around the object, grasping at anything she could use as she struggled against the crushing blackness.

It was Gran's crucifix.

Focus. Feel.

Balance soon followed.

She stopped fighting against the need for air and control, allowing her body to drift with the current.

She surfaced, gasping for air, and opened her eyes to a looming iceberg.

Only the polestar kept it company above the empty sea.

The iceberg's tip was blinding white and pristine, while the lower section at the water level had veins of black streaking upward, seeking to devour it.

On its face, there must have been a ledge as she focused on the form of a bear, clinging and exhausted.

Ana swam toward it, as much as she could, through the thickening black mire, sucking at her legs to drag her back under.

She trembled against the cold as her body threatened to seize.

Not now! Not now.

"Aksel!" she screamed without stopping.

The bear turned its weary head in her direction but didn't move.

The downward drag on her body nearly had her below the surface again. Panic flared through her, but the crucifix in her palm reminded her to focus.

Shivering, she focused on relaxing her body, feeling the direction of the water—the actual water not the inky oil slick that tainted it and surrounded the iceberg.

Water was Ana's natural element. It was her emotional conduit. She sought it now to enable her to reach Aksel.

She opened her eyes when her shoulder bumped into something smooth and solid.

Aksel peered down at her from his ledge.

Her hand slipped off the icy surface as the current threatened to sweep her right past him.

His paw slapped the side of the iceberg, claws anchored in the ice so Ana could pull herself out of the water.

After several minutes of struggling, she climbed his furry arm and collapsed next to him, chest heaving.

"Thanks."

He huffed.

"I'm with Magnus," she finally said.

He didn't move or make any effort to shift in order to communicate with her.

"Are you in bear form to stay warm, or are you stuck like that?"

This time, his huff contained a despondent growl.

His morose state rippled over her.

Pushing herself into a seated position, she placed a hand on his damp, dirty fur. "We're going to try to help you. But we need you to help us figure out how."

The next huff *felt* like a sardonic laugh.

"Where are we?"

He turned his head, leveling his gaze on her, one polar bear brow raised.

"Yeah, fucked if I know too," she said, uncharacteristically using the 'F' word as she surveyed the empty ocean. "Okay, listen Aksel. We found you aboard a cargo ship, hidden in the engine room, badly beaten and unconscious. That's all we know. That and that you have a sigil tattoo at the base of your throat. We need to know what happened to you and anything you can tell us about the mark. So, if you could take your human form and explain it all, that'd be totally awesome."

The bear stared at her, and she had the distinct feeling he wanted to chomp her head.

"Fair enough, but if you eat me, I can't help you."

The next impression was something like, '*how the hell can* you *help me?*'

Going with the hunch, she said, "I'm guessing you'd like to know how I'm going to help you. Well, whether you're aware or not, we are not physically on this iceberg in the middle of the ocean. We're somewhere in your psyche. Your body is in a comfy hospital bed with IV's hooked up to you. Magnus is standing by and worried about you."

There was no response as she stared the polar bear in the face.

His nose twitched, scenting.

Then he shoved her shoulder with his snout.

Who the hell are *you?*

How much should she tell him? Could this sigil link somehow convey information back to its originator?

Maybe she'd already said too much.

"My name is Ana. I'm able to reach you through my psychic ability."

Shaman.

"Sort of, but not really. I don't have the skills and experience your shaman would."

She considered what she knew of shamanic wisdom, which wasn't much, and realized that maybe that's what he needed—his clan shaman.

"Is that what you want? Do you want us to take you to your shaman?"

He growled.

"Oh, oh dear, okay, that was a clear 'no'. But why not?"

Why wouldn't Aksel want to go to the shaman?

She sat next to him, arse frozen to the iceberg as she tried to work through the problems and frustrated that he couldn't just communicate with her in plain English. Then she realized she didn't even know if Aksel spoke English, anyway.

But he understood her.

Because they were in his psyche.

And yet, even here, he was trapped in his bear, while his physical body remained trapped in his human.

She dropped her face into her hands. This was way beyond her pay grade. None of this was anything Maeda had ever worked on with her. They'd never gotten this far.

Because usually, she grew tired and lost her connection.

How long had she been here already? Was she trapped here, too?

Oh, dear God, that would be so bad.

Tell me about it.

She popped her head up and looked at Aksel. "You can hear my thoughts?"

He dipped his head with a little tilt.

Her body shuddered against the cold, her hand gripping Gran's crucifix.

No, she wouldn't be trapped. But that didn't mean she should stay here any longer than she needed to.

She had an idea.

From this ledge, they could only see in one direction. Maybe, just maybe, the open ocean wasn't all Aksel had access to here.

She stood, stretching out her stiffening joints, and flexed her hands against the cold.

Ana tried to find a place to climb. There weren't many footholds on the face of the ice. Most of it was too slick for her to grip.

"Aksel. Can you help me get to the top of your iceberg?"

He turned his head, looking up to its snowy peak beyond the black veins creeping up from the ocean. Now that she watched them for a few moments, she noticed they continued to creep upward—consuming.

A wave of sudden dizziness overwhelmed her, causing her to stumble as she tried to step onto a more solid spot.

The black, oozing water pooled around her feet, impeding her ability to ascend.

Aksel's fur was covered in the stuff. Did it weigh him down too?

"We have to try, Aksel. I need you to help me *see* more."

If there is anything more to see.

They both thought it.

But he looked down at his paws. The water encroached on him too. He stood and staggered forward.

The water seemed to reach for him, to drag him back.

He looked down at it, then seemed to notice how it coated his fur. He engaged in a full body shake to dislodge the blackened water from his body.

It flew off in a cloudy spray, splattering the iceberg and open water beyond.

Some of it gathered itself, pooling and oozing back toward Aksel's paws.

He climbed.

Ana struggled to climb alongside him but couldn't get a grip.

On.

"Climb *you*?"

He huffed and repositioned his rear leg and dug the claws into the ice so that she could use it.

"Okay, if you insist," she said with a last glance at the black puddles that seemed to try to find them through the dips and valleys in the ice.

Once she was on, she gripped his fur in her fists and tried not to put her knees and feet in awkward places to impede his ability to reach the summit.

The higher they went, the heavier the pressure on her mind.

Aksel felt it too.

She felt it in the way he struggled to move ever upward, his sides laboring with the effort.

But finally, finally, they crested the iced peak and Aksel dug his claws in so as not to slide back down to where he'd worked so hard to climb from.

"Oh, my god." Ana breathed.

Beyond them, the sea was filled with dozens, if not hundreds, of other icebergs of all shapes and sizes and in various states of being consumed by the black water, turning the ice and snow to varying shades of white, gray and black.

There were a few more polar bears occupying other icebergs. There were also humans—many of them. A few other creatures occupied the floating surfaces.

They floated between two visible coast lines, small ports on either side.

The inky water stretched between the two land masses; the land as streaked with black as the ink burrowed like seeking vines.

Then she understood.

They *were* all connected.

They were all connected by the black, inky magic of this sigil.

"We have to somehow break the sigil."

But how?

TWELVE

ANA GROANED AND MAGNUS instantly lunged forward to scoop her up from the floor.

She was small and limp in his arms as he strode out of Aksel's room, seeking any other room where he could lay her on a comfortable surface.

"This way." Kane led him to a nearby sitting room with plump couches.

He gently laid Ana on one, placing her shoulders on the padded arm, and reached for a cushion to prop behind her.

Her eyes fluttered open, searching the room around her as her body trembled.

"I'm... it's so... cold." Her teeth chattered.

"I'll get some hot tea—get her warmed up," Kane said, leaving the room.

Magnus pulled Ana forward and slid behind her so that her back was to his chest and wrapped his arms around her, much like he'd done that first night in the hangar.

"Aksel... so many..." she struggled to get the words out. "Connected. Consuming..."

"Just rest right now," he murmured against the top of her head, relieved to have her back. He bundled her closer, reaching across the back of the couch for a wool throw to tuck around her.

By the time Kane returned bearing a tray with a teapot and mugs, Ana's trembling had settled into random little shivers.

Kane selected a steaming mug and crouched next to the couch. "Ana." Her voice was soft, encouraging Ana to look at her.

After a moment, Ana's head, resting on Magnus' chest, tilted so she could look at Kane.

"I brought your phone."

"Turn the recorder on," Ana murmured as she reached for the hot tea. "Thank you."

She recited everything she saw and felt in Aksel's mind.

Kane and Magnus listened, steaming mugs in hand.

Magnus' heart dropped at her descriptions of Aksel's isolation and the view she described of all the other icebergs, both with more of his kinsmen and other victims.

She said they were all connected.

Where are they all?

"What does it all mean?" he asked when she finished.

"I'm really not sure, Magnus. But, he emphatically didn't want me to go to the clan shaman for help." She sighed. "I'm sorry. I didn't get anything useful out of all that."

"What can you tell us about the shaman, Magnus?" Kane asked, refilling his mug.

He shrugged. "The shaman that I knew growing up was my father's closest friend and advisor. His duty was to oversee all royal rituals and activities, but above all, to protect the king from non-physical threats. He had a Guardian Chief for the physical ones. I haven't seen him or anyone else from Barentia since they banished me. I haven't been back, and I haven't had any contact with anyone—not even my son."

Ana jerked in his arms, sitting up and moving away so she could turn to look at him, her expression incredulous. "You have a son? You have a son you haven't seen in a decade?"

"Yes," he said, his body tensing.

She frowned as she considered this, but said nothing more about it. Instead, she turned to Kane. "Why do you want us to go into his clan's territory?"

Kane looked at Magnus.

"Joey, she should know," Magnus said to Kane, using her given name, which he rarely did.

"Know what?" Ana demanded.

Wearily, Joey held Magnus' gaze before turning her attention to Ana. "It's my fault Magnus was banished."

"I wouldn't say it was *your* fault," Magnus objected.

"It was. Is. If I hadn't pushed your father so hard, he probably wouldn't have turned against you when you tried to help make him see reason about the prophecies."

Magnus snorted. "Maybe. But there were also an awful lot of underlying clan politics that pushed him toward his decision."

"Prophecies?"

A pang struck Magnus when Ana moved away from him, renewing the distance between them as she slid to the opposite end of the couch. She huddled in the wool throw he'd wrapped around her.

He turned so that both his feet were firmly on the floor, elbows on his knees, as they continued their discussion.

"Look, Joey, you've always known something was going to happen there. That was the whole deal in the first place. Something is happening and we need to find out how it relates." He rubbed his hands over his beard and through his hair. "How else would Aksel end up on a human trafficking ship with a hex tattooed into his throat like this?"

Magnus had never seen Joey with any kind of expression that resembled uncertainty before.

"Why are you back-peddling now? Why *now*, when you were just pushing us to move forward on this yesterday?" he demanded. "We're so close, Joey. *So* close."

"Is it because of the shaman? And what's this about prophecies?" Ana asked again, setting her mug on the floor next to the couch.

"Yes. The way forward isn't as clear to me now. I need to think this through. We'll discuss the prophecies later, but it's all part of the reason Magnus needs to go to Barentia."

Ana cut in. "If we can somehow break the sigil, wouldn't that free Aksel? Then he could wake up and just tell us what we need to know? That black inky stuff seemed to consume the icebergs and I don't know what that means for him—or the others."

"It's not so simple as that." Joey's voice was gentle as she reached a hand to Ana's knee. "Even if there was some way to remove the tattoo, it magically embedded the ink in his skin and bloodstream."

"Magic like that has very few counteragents."

"Death is usually the main one," Magnus said, "Of the creator, or the recipient."

"Are there any other tattooed victims nearby that I could interview? I might get more information from someone that is trapped in human form," Ana asked.

Joey shook her head. "They're all being cared for at facilities close to their homes, although GPSA is monitoring them and keeping us informed."

Ana threw off the blanket as she stood, then began pacing. "Okay, I really don't think I can do anything useful with my gifts. But at the very least, I *can* pose as Magnus' fiancée if that gets him through the door, and close to whomever he needs to talk to. Since I can't actually help save anyone, this is the very least I can do." She paused mid stride and shrugged. "If it's a dead end, then we move on. Who knows, maybe this will give Magnus a chance to see his son."

Magnus blinked. He cleared the sudden lump in his throat. "That would be irrelevant to the mission."

"Like hell it is," Ana exploded, color blooming in her cheeks. "Sons need their fathers. Fathers need their children. You—." She closed her eyes, straightened her spine and drew a breath. "Everyone has the right to see their family."

A smile tugged at Magnus' lips. "That's not exactly how my society works, but I appreciate the sentiment, Ana."

"I can feel it, Magnus," she said, impassioned, her fist over her heart.

Magnus' gaze darted to Joey, who studied Ana closely.

His heart thudded in his chest, his emotions and thoughts tumbling between Ana and his clan—his family.

My god, she is beautiful when she is unrestrained.

The idea that he might see his son... after all this time.

Fear iced his spine.

He'd avoided thoughts along that path over the years. It did no good to entertain them.

Banished meant erased, in most cases.

The only reason he'd possibly be allowed back at all was only because he was the king's son, and his bloodline needed to be tracked. Hence the recording of unions and offspring.

A decade had passed since he'd last set eyes on his tiny boy. He'd be approaching manhood now. Still a boy, but not for much longer.

As quickly as the thoughts appeared, he brushed them away again.

That way was dangerous. To his heart, and his soul.

There was no room in Magnus' life for family. Not anymore.

I won't go through that again.

No, best to focus on the mission. Always the mission.

The bigger picture.

He would go, just as he'd been prepared to when Kane had first ordered it.

And he would banish thoughts of seeing his son from his mind.

If he didn't, he might not leave again.

He would fail the mission, because he'd take his son with him this time, which would incite a war that would ruin everything.

ANA DUG THROUGH HER two open suitcases, seeking the warmest of her warm clothing.

Seated on the floor between them, damp hair piled on top of her head, thin robe loosely belted around her freshly showered body, she groaned.

Right back where she started. Stressing and panicked over what to wear.

But this was different.

So different.

Iceland wasn't like Barentia.

Iceland was cold, yes, but it also had people. People that she might turn to for help, should something go wrong.

Ana laughed.

She was fucked.

So. Fucked.

She'd panicked over Iceland, was relieved to land in Ireland... and now?

Iceland was a cakewalk compared to Barentia.

Barentia would eat her alive.

Literally.

An ancient civilization of Northmen and women, never tamed like the rest of the world. Insular and strong in their brutal ways.

No, that was unfair.

She thought of Magnus.

He wasn't brutal at all. As far as she'd experienced so far, he was more... gentle teddy bear than fierce wild northern polar bear.

Even when she'd ranted at him like an idiot.

God, what an idiot.

She sighed, throwing her cotton underwear back onto a pile she'd already moved several times.

She eyed the segregated pile of lace and satin thongs and bras she normally wore.

Definitely not practical.

But her favorites.

She sighed, picking up the small pile, trying to decide what to do with them when there was a knock on her door.

"Come in." She got to her feet, expecting a member of the household staff come to deliver a message from Kane.

Magnus stepped inside, closing the door behind him, quickly surveyed the disaster, eyes landing on the cluster of thongs dangling from her fingers.

Ana couldn't whip her hand behind her back fast enough.

She blushed when a thick blond brow rose over his twinkling blue-grey eyes.

She cleared her throat. "How can I help you?"

The corner of his mouth quirked as his expression turned mischievous. "Pack light—but maybe not too light, you'll want to be warm. Wheels up at six."

"Six!" Ana spun around, assessing her mess. "Just how cold will it be?"

When Magnus stepped close enough to peer over the mess, she had to resist the urge to lean back into his warm, wonderful smelling personal space, but it was hard.

He always smelled so good, and it seemed the more often she caught a whiff of whatever scent he wore, the more she wanted to sniff him.

And with it, came the recollection of how wonderful it felt to have his arms around her.

She tilted her head, turning enough to look up into his bearded face as he considered her piles of clothes.

Long, thick blond hair loosely braided back from his face. Deep-set eyes, and a straight nose over full lips, framed by his impressive beard. His grooming was impeccable, he smelled amazing and he just... enveloped her in a cocoon of security when he was so close.

She wanted more of that. More of him.

Her gaze swept his wide shoulders and thick biceps.

Her palms itched to explore his muscled arms, the ridges and valleys of his torso... and more.

Her eyes sought his lips, remembered that kiss in the hallway the previous night, and how it had left her wanting so much more.

She bit her lip. Did he want more of her, too?

That kiss... left her with the impression that he might.

"I don't see much that's appropriate for Barentia temperatures. We'll just have to make sure you stay close so I can keep you safe and warm."

"Safe and warm?" she repeated as his words made their way through the haze of distracted visual exploration she'd been engaged in. She blinked, turning toward him.

Ana looked up at Magnus, his eyes locked on her lips.

Her breath hitched as her face tilted up toward his.

"I'm partial to blue," his low voice rippled through her.

"Blue?" She licked her lips, inching toward him, mesmerized.

A light tug drew her attention to the hand that still clutched her forgotten underwear. A sapphire blue satin thong dangled from Magnus' forefinger.

Ana's cheeks flamed. Desire swept down her body, pooling at her core. Her nipples peaked as she stepped closer still.

Chest tight against the overwhelming desire, she sucked in a breath, dragging his delicious scents into her.

She'd never been sensitive to scents before, but it seemed she was becoming intoxicated by him. She couldn't get enough.

Magnus' warm hand slid behind the edge of her silk robe, pulling her to him.

She gasped as their chests collided.

He took advantage of her open mouth, slipping his tongue across the tip of hers between her parted lips, inciting sparks of erotic sensations all over her body.

She crackled.

Her fingers shook as raw desire raged through her, surprising the logical part of her brain, which seemed so very far away now.

What was it about Magnus that made her feel so primal?

She wasn't a shifter. She didn't have those instincts.

Do I?

His lips left hers as he nibbled his way along her jaw to her throat.

She bared it to him. Her fingers clasped his arms for support as she pressed her body into his.

The sensation of his beard along her sensitive flesh made her shudder and groan as he inhaled her scent.

His large hand slid down her back to grip her bottom as he pulled her against his steely erection behind the barrier of his jeans.

Desire slammed through her, stealing her breath away.

What's happening?

One moment she was sorting clothes, the next she was throwing herself at a man she'd only known for a few days.

A colleague, her small, logical brain, reminded her.

This isn't me.

Is it?

Her robe fell from her shoulders, leaving only the thin night dress which barely covered the tops of her thighs.

Nothing else.

Magnus leaned back, one hand still on her rear, locking her in place so that she could feel his hard length and he could feel her moist heat.

The other hand cradled her cheek and jaw. "You're so beautiful." He murmured, gaze fluttering over her features.

Her hands dropped to his waist, tugging at his shirt, desperate to press her palms to his hot flesh.

"Kiss me, Magnus." It was more a breath than a whisper.

Her brain screamed '*make love to me'.*

She had wanted it since she saw him that first night and buried it; like everything else she wanted.

He growled as his lips descended to hers.

Like the night before, the rumble of his growl shot straight to her core.

Her hands slid down. She unbuckled his belt before attacking his jeans, to free him in seconds as her hand slid behind the waistband of his boxers to grip his rigid length.

His growl deepened and the erotic need surged through her, gripping him hard and stroking.

He pulled his shirt up over his head, tossing it to the floor among her clothes.

Her hands shoved at his jeans. The boxers fell with them.

She stared at the sight of him, tongue darting over her lips as he pulsed with need.

Her gaze rose to meet the hunger in his eyes.

Would he devour her?

THIRTEEN

MAGNUS STARED INTO ANA'S dark eyes, liquid with desire. Her scent enticed his animal brain, so that there was only her.

She was killing him every time her gaze explored his body, tongue peeking out between her plump lips. He wanted nothing more than to feel the flutter of that little pink tongue and soft lips all over his body.

Soon enough, but not yet.

He dragged a breath into his lungs. The scent of her arousal enveloped both of them, and he'd barely touched her.

Mine.

Ana is mine.

Mate.

His mate. The fact had locked in place when their lips met the previous night.

There was no longer any doubt in his mind. She was *his*.

Magnus wasn't sure she'd reached that conclusion—yet.

But, he also had to ensure that she knew he was hers too.

He grinned down at her barely controlled restraint.

Her self-control only seemed to slip when she was around him.

Magnus wanted Ana to lose all of it.

By the time they left for Barentia in the morning, they would be covered in each other's scents.

There would be no more doubt for either of them, and certainly none for anyone else that might challenge their claims to each other's bodies—or their hearts.

She didn't know she already held his in her small hands.

Ana was the psychic one, but Magnus knew things too.

He knew, like nothing he'd ever known in his life, that she would cherish it like the fragile ice sculpture that it had become after Ulla had forced him out of his home.

Magnus also understood that as big as her heart was, so full of compassion and kindness, it was just as fragile as his own. And she wouldn't easily give it over. She trusted him, but not enough.

"What are you grinning at?" she demanded, brow furrowed.

"You. You're a wild hell cat and you don't even know it."

Ana snorted, stepping back, indignant. "I am not."

He shrugged, his grin widening. "If you say so."

She eyed him suspiciously as he leaned in to claim her lips again.

His tongue swiped her lip, eliciting a low moan. She leaned into his chest, forcing him back against the wall as though the mere mention of the word 'wild' had unlocked something in her.

Her roaming hands found his chest and abdomen, sliding ever lower.

He caught her hands before they gripped him again. Linking his fingers through hers, he spun them around, pressed her back to the wall, and pinned her hands against its surface above her head.

The motion pushed her breasts up. Her hips fell forward, pressing against his, rubbing his hard cock between their bodies.

He stilled against the sudden near-loss of his own control.

Little minx.

Magnus deepened their kiss. She grew supple against him before he moved downward, grazing his lips over her silk-covered skin, earning little gasps as he went. He nuzzled and nibbled each breast, then the valley between, dragging his nose along the flat expanse of her belly, downward still.

His hands gripped her hips as he crouched before her. Her fingers clutched his shoulders as she stared down into his face, her breath in little puffs between her parted lips.

The grin returned to Magnus' mouth as he dragged the silk up from her thighs.

Palms on his shoulders, lifting herself away from his seeking mouth, she twisted in his grasp. She squeaked, "Magnus, I—."

But he hushed her with a breath against the sensitive, exposed flesh below her belly button and above her mound, where he placed a kiss before looking up into her wide eyes, staring down at him.

Through his mounting desire, he registered her panicked expression at her naked vulnerability.

She's never been properly worshiped.

With all the gentleness in his being, Magnus slid his tongue and lips over little spots on her thigh, working his way back up to her hip and across her belly.

When he glanced up again, her head had fallen back against the wall, although the pressure on his shoulders hadn't eased.

She was afraid.

Not of him.

She read others. He read *her*.

Lips pressed to her lower belly, he murmured, ever so softly, ever so low. "Open for me, sweetheart." Then his tongue circled her belly button before placing another kiss.

She moaned.

Her arms trembled as she struggled against herself, her fingers gripping his shoulders.

He looked up into her flushed face, holding her gaze. Her lower lip caught between her teeth.

His cock jerked. He ignored it.

She must have seen it because just then, the corner of her mouth curled.

Dear gods, she was sexy as all hell, and Magnus wanted nothing more than to bury himself deep inside her.

Emboldened by her effect on him, she turned so that he had full access to what he wanted.

Magnus loved how her breath still came in little pants of anticipation.

He inhaled, drawing her scent deeper still, before he placed the tenderest of kisses to her hot, moist center.

She shuddered at the contact, breath hissing through her teeth.

His tongue flicked over her, causing her arms to buckle.

Ana caught herself against the wall, palms flat.

Magnus slid a hand up her ankle, along her calf, lifting her knee over his shoulder.

Looking up into her face, he held her gaze as he lowered his mouth and set to devour her properly.

Ana hissed. Her nails scratched at the wall. She growled and spat. And she screamed as she came.

He lapped it all up.

Her body trembled around him.

Easing her foot back to the floor, he swept her limp form into his arms and finally carried her to the bed, where he continued to lick and kiss every inch of her.

He couldn't get enough of her. The more he tasted, the more he wanted.

By the time he slid into her, he'd ensured that she understood they belonged to one another.

As he moved inside of her, she rose to meet him, pulling him in deeper and deeper.

Claiming him.

Magnus' eyes locked on Ana's as she crested again. He gave her everything that he was, as they toppled over the edge in each other's arms.

She claimed his mouth one last time and released him with a grin.

"You wanted a hellcat. You got one."

He chuckled against her mouth before he rolled them to the side, wrapped his arms around her, and watched her beautiful face until she fell asleep.

BEFORE DAWN, MAGNUS ROUSED Ana from her languid slumber.

She groaned, rolling out of the bed, her feet slapping the floor on her way to the shower.

Ten minutes later, Magnus was nowhere to be seen. She found a backpack containing her clothes and anything else she would need for the trip. The rest of her belongings were neatly replaced in her suitcases and pushed aside.

She quickly dressed in the clothes set beside the pack, dried her hair and tied it back.

A knock at her door drew her attention. She opened it to find one of the household staff delivering a pair of insulated boots and a much better jacket than the one she had.

"From Mistress Kane. There is food for you and Mr. Bjornson in the breakfast room."

She glanced at her watch before accepting the boots and coat. "Thank you," she said, closing the door.

Ana quickly slipped the boots on and laced them up. One last glance around the room, noting the wild state of the bed sheets and blanket, she tugged them back into place and plumped the pillows.

Grabbing the coat and pack, she left for the breakfast room, trying not to think about all the things they'd done in that bed just hours before.

All of *that* would have to wait.

There was work to do.

FOURTEEN

Magnus glanced at the dials and adjusted a few settings on the cockpit panel.

Next to him, Ana occupied the co-pilot's chair, tense but quiet. At least she didn't have a mask over her lovely eyes this time.

She tentatively glanced out of the window again, each time for a little longer.

And when the sun crested the horizon, her gasp of awe sent a thrum through his heart.

The view from well above bird's eye was incredible. One reason he loved flying.

The other, the speed and danger-control factor, was also the reason he enjoyed driving fast cars and motorcycles.

Something Ana would learn about in time.

He cast her another glance, wondering what he would learn about her?

Soon, she relaxed and spent most of her time peering down from her side window.

"That's Norway below us?"

"Yes, we'll be landing on the easterly tip then going the rest of the way by amphibious plane. Barentia doesn't have a landing strip."

She nodded.

"What do I need to know about Barentia?"

"Stay close. There won't be a warm welcome. I'll find an excuse to stay at least a day or two. You're not a polar bear, or even a shifter, so expect some intimidation."

She nodded.

"Don't be afraid to make your taser visible. Keep your hand-gun well hidden."

Her fingers drummed her knee as she looked down at the ocean and mountains.

"What are these prophecies that Kane mentioned?"

Magnus sighed. He was the one that had said Ana had a right to know. But Kane hadn't offered any more on the subject. "It's best if she explains it all."

"Cliffs' notes?"

"Kane's been around a long time. *Long* time. And she's been collecting information about ancient prophecies. That's why she came to Barentia in the first place. She believed there was a link between my homeland and the information she was studying."

"Which is?"

Magnus shrugged. "She and my father and the old shaman had long, long discussions on the matter. Something to do with a gateway of sorts."

"What does this have to do with the trafficking ring we're investigating?"

"Nothing. Everything." He rubbed a hand over his face. "She asked for two things. Help with the prophecies and help fighting against the growing practice of shifters exploiting humans. My father sent her away and told me never to deal with her when he was gone—when I became king of the clan. Barentians never get involved with human affairs. When I pushed him on it, he said that we would do as we'd always done; keep to our own and shut the world out. That I wasn't ready yet. The shaman said little on the matter, beyond how vital it was that we protect our territory, to keep the darkness away."

"Sounds very cryptic."

"Yeah, well, my father was incensed that I went to talk to Kane myself and find out what she had to say on the matter. Her view was that whatever was coming, every civilization had a responsibility to fight against those that would use this darkness which the shaman had mentioned. Made sense to me."

"Your father disagreed."

Magnus nodded. "We continued to argue in the following weeks and months. Kane tried again. He demanded she never return. I, being young and impatient, challenged him. Turns out Ulla also disagreed with my viewpoint, and had been putting words in my father's ear. There was another heir—my son. The clan didn't need me."

Magnus gave his attention to the flight gauges for a few moments, to shake the lingering emotions for his ex-wife.

Ana maintained her silence.

"Uphold our insular traditions, or go. The Clan or Kane. My heart said to stay and shut the fuck up. My gut told me I had to go."

It was far, far more complicated than that.

"You trust her? More than your father?"

Magnus shrugged. "Instinct."

She didn't ask why he didn't just wait out his father's rule, or why he chose a stranger over his family—his son.

He'd had a decade to study his choices. Swallow his regrets.

To work with Kane, even though his absence from Barentia meant she didn't have the ally she'd sought *in* that territory.

Some days, it felt like it was all for nothing.

Considering the struggle to protect humans from exploitive paranormals, Magnus had done a lot, but it wasn't enough.

"So, you're not welcome. Humans aren't welcome. They know we're agents."

"They know *I* work for the GPSA. They may assume the same of you, or not. But as a human, they can't automatically assume you're a threat of any kind. Anyone else would put them on their guard."

Magnus flicked several switches and began their descent toward land.

"Ready?"

"As I'll ever be."

FEAR POUNDED THROUGH ANA'S chest as they left the seaplane tied to a simple dock and began the trek up the snow-covered path toward the fishing village.

Somewhere on the eastern tip of Norway, they'd landed and switched to the smaller amphibious aircraft for the rest of the journey.

She struggled to control her heart rate.

Pulling her phone from her pocket, she checked for cell service, holding it up in various directions, trying to catch *something*.

They would smell her fear, making her an easy target.

She laughed at herself, tucking her phone away.

She was already an easy target. A human on an island full of powerful shifters, but she also wasn't helpless. Her fingers ghosted over her weapons before she drew a breath. On its release, she opened her senses.

Time to get to work.

Barentia, like everywhere else in this part of the globe, was comprised of mountainous islands rising out of the steely waters of the north. The world was all shades of gray and blue, white and black, with little variety in between. Even the coniferous trees appeared more black than green.

Without looking at her, Magnus reached out to squeeze her glove-covered hand as several villagers came out to see who'd interrupted their daily routine of coastal life.

Magnus' name drifted between individuals until a stoic older woman emerged from the gathering crowd of astonished faces.

Surprise, disdain, and hostility rippled through the air.

Magnus' appearance pleased some villagers, but you wouldn't know it to look at their craggy, sea-worn faces.

She felt it.

They looked from Magnus to Ana, and moved aside.

The old woman stood at the top of the path. She looked like any of the other villagers. Magnus stopped before her, head bowed.

Ana didn't understand Barentian, but through observing their facial expressions, body language and psychic energy, she got the gist of what was going on.

Magnus and the older woman exchanged a few words before she turned her back on them. Magnus followed her. Ana followed him.

The elder woman led them to an ornately carved wooden structure where a boy awaited her. With a few sharp words from the woman, the boy's gaze darted between her, Magnus and Ana, then he set off like an Olympic sprinter along another path that led away from the ocean.

Magnus whispered to Ana as he held the door opened for her to precede him inside the building. "The boy will send a message to alert my father that we have arrived."

Moving into the space felt like stepping into an energy cloud. The hairs on her arms rose.

Magnus whispered close to her ear. "As a banished one, I'm not welcome in resident's homes, but the temple is a place open to all."

With Ana's senses open, and the high energy of the place, Magnus' proximity made her skin tingle even through the layers of clothing until he stepped away again.

She nodded, gaze sweeping the beautifully crafted interior lit by braziers. At the far end of the open space, an altar filled the far wall.

The village temple. The woman was no doubt its priestess.

Ana approached the altar. Touching nothing, she inspected the symbols and offerings.

None looked anything like the sigil imprinted on Aksel's throat.

The elder appeared next to her.

Ana turned toward her, met and held her gaze before offering her hand. "I'm Analiese Ortega."

"Beyla Jorgansdotter." The woman shook her hand with a firm grip. The corner of her thin lips tilted upward as she assessed Ana. With a short laugh, she turned toward a table with a pitcher and glasses, speaking to Magnus over her shoulder as she poured.

"She says I've brought you here to clean up my mess," Magnus said.

"What is she talking about?"

Magnus relayed the question and translated the elder's answer.

"She says things haven't been the same since I left the clan. My father is different. More conflict among Barentians than is usual. And in recent years, a gang seems to have formed."

"A gang?"

"Young Barentians rove from village to village, recruiting the strongest among them to join their gang, and off they go." He paused, listening as the elder continued to talk. "At first, they thought the king was forming an additional guard to protect the territory from what the priests and priestesses knew was the coming darkness, but it seems not to be the case."

"What *are* they doing?"

She shrugged. "No good," she said in English, her accent thick as she handed them each a glass.

Ana sniffed at the liquid.

"Barentian ale," Magnus said with a smile. He drank the entire glass. "Ah, I've missed this stuff."

"What did she mean, your father is different?" Ana took a tentative sip.

"I assume it means he's accepting outsiders to the island now, since we weren't met at spear point when we arrived at the dock."

"Except that's what you argued about and were banished for?"

Magnus nodded.

"That doesn't make sense."

"No, it doesn't."

Heavy footsteps sounded outside the door before it opened. The young boy appeared, chest heaving, speaking between breaths.

"He notified the relay. We can go," Magnus said.

Ana turned to offer her thanks to the woman for her hospitality.

The elder went to the altar, glanced along its surface and retrieved an artifact, cradling it on her palm as she returned to Magnus and Ana.

The elder reached for Ana's hand, surprising her.

Magnus translated her words. "Don't let the darkness touch your heart when it comes; but even the light can be a barrier.

And when it's imperative to open your heart, the bear will be your polestar."

Ana looked at the talisman in her hand. A polar bear carved in polished ivory. Flipping it over, she studied the etched symbol on its back. The top of the talisman had a drilled hole with a metal link so it could be worn on a necklace or bracelet.

"Thank you," she said, pulling Gran's rosary and crucifix from her pocket while the woman continued to speak to Magnus directly. Ana attached the bear talisman next to the crucifix, considering it. She was about to tuck it all back into her pocket when, instead, she looped it around her wrist and tucked it under her shirt cuff.

Maybe it's just the weird warning about light and dark.

Or how the village elder reminded her of her grandmother.

Or something else entirely that Ana couldn't define.

Priestess Beyla Jorgansdotter led Magnus and Ana back out of the temple so that they might continue their journey.

The villagers had remained outside all that time, and observed their departure inland. Their somber faces, hopeful auras, and the elder's strange warnings coiled through Ana, twisting up her insides, adding to her deep unease about this mission.

Despite the mention of outsiders no longer denied access to Barentian territory, she doubted an extraction team could rescue them, should things go wrong—as her gut told her they inevitably would.

FIFTEEN

DURING THE LONG WALK, Magnus ruminated over what the village elder had told him.

Everything about Barentia *looked* the same.

Everything about Barentia *felt* different.

Subtle differences that would be a trickle-down effect from their leader.

Why would his father change his stance on outsiders, especially after he'd done the extreme act of banishing his only son and direct heir?

"They don't look it, Magnus, but I could feel that many of them are pleased to see you." Ana had said to him as they left the village boundary behind them.

Her words should have made him feel better.

They didn't.

He noted how quiet the road was between the coastal village and his father's stronghold.

A stronghold that didn't seem necessary to a culture of polar bear shifters that had rejected most outsiders for the last few centuries.

Mostly human outsiders, of course. And most other paranormals that weren't polar bear shifters like themselves, which were usually vetted before setting foot in the territory.

Like his former wife, Ulla, and her younger brother, Aksel; children of the ruler of the Novaya Zemlya clan that occupied the Matochkin strait, whom it was named for.

A political alliance.

Although they deterred most outsiders, there were still rival clans that would seek to conquer and control Barentia for their own gain.

Hence, the massive stone stronghold that housed Magnus' forebears.

Other clans had tried and failed to take it over. Barentia had always been too strong.

They'd been strong because they'd kept their borders tight. Easier to do when you occupied a frozen archipelago in a northern ocean.

Unease slithered at Magnus' nape.

The elder had said Bjorn Thornsson was different. He didn't look out for his people as he once had. They hadn't seen him in a long time because there hadn't been a gathering or festival in years.

Magnus had been gone for a decade.

Barentia, like a glacier, was slow to change. Annual gatherings and festivals were a vital activity in their way of life.

What other changes would he see when they reached his former home?

He glanced at Ana, walking alongside him, bundled in borrowed cold-weather gear. With her face framed in a faux-fur trim, the tip of her nose was pink, and her cheeks bloomed under the pale blue sky.

Magnus wore his usual clothes, with the addition of an extra layer under his leather jacket.

They both bore backpacks with more clothing and supplies.

He frowned, recalling the elder's cryptic words to Ana. She clearly sensed there was more to her.

But then, she'd been cryptic about everything she'd said.

At first, Magnus attributed it to the fact that he was a returned banished, and he should have been shunned by all he met.

It was the way.

He had expected resistance at their arrival, and had been surprised they'd allowed him off the dock, let alone parted for him to enter the village and their most sacred space.

They had all remained silent.

The elder had chosen her words carefully.

Like someone could be listening.

IT WAS LONG DARK by the time they reached the foot of the fortress built into the base of the island's weathered mountain.

They had exchanged few words, preferring to focus energy on the journey.

"Cozy," Ana muttered, "Don't suppose it has indoor plumbing and a reliable heating system?"

"If they don't send us away immediately, they'll probably relegate us to a hut outside the town's boundary. *If* we're lucky. More likely, we'll be sleeping in the tent that I have bundled in my pack."

Ana groaned, her expression pleading that it wasn't the case.

"Don't worry, I know many ways to keep you warm." He winked and saw that she couldn't help but smile.

"Shall we get this over with?"

Magnus nodded. The smile dropped from his face as he stepped forward.

Toward his past.

Toward the father that banished him from his world.

The ex-wife that had undermined him.

The son that no longer knew him.

The rest of his friends and family that had all turned their backs on him.

None had protested the banishment. None had come forward for him. He'd been alone. Until he joined Kane's Organization. What else was there for him?

He'd questioned everything in those days; Kane, her motives, her sanity. Others that worked for her. In time, he'd learned to trust her, as his instinct had urged him to do, but he still questioned her regularly. As he'd done with his father. It was in his nature.

Unlike his father, Joey Kane respected him for it.

When did it all go wrong?

He sighed, staring up at the familiar stone walls built into the mountainside.

As far as he could recall, everything changed after the birth of his son, Elias.

It should have been a happy time, full of wonder and rightness—and it was, for a little while. His world revolved around his brand-new little cub. He'd never experienced pride and love like that before. Magnus held those memories deeply buried under the permafrost, protecting his heart.

Everyone changed.

While at the time it was difficult to discern what was happening and who was instigating the direction of things, time and distance had since made it easier to see what was happening.

Ulla.

Still, Magnus was cautious where to lay the blame, despite how contentious their separation had been.

Family break-ups were messy, and everyone had some responsibility to claim.

A decade was a long time.

As Ana passed through the smaller door set into the massive iron-banded wooden gates, she remembered to keep her mouth closed as she took in her surroundings—she was so in awe of the place.

She breathed a sigh of relief as the high walls blocked the arctic wind from freezing her through to her bones. She didn't care that Magnus insisted it wasn't winter. She'd already decided she'd never, ever, be in the arctic during that particular season. The current climate was bad enough.

They stood between two stone walls, lined with snow and ice in every crevice and cranny. The ground, clear of either, was surfaced with a stone road and a cobbled foot path.

She gave a little laugh. "This place is incredible. It reminds me of a dwarven mountain castle from the movies."

"That's because we worked together to build the place."

Ana stumbled on the cobbles. "Wait-what? Dwarves are *real?* You're joking, right? This place has to have been built centuries ago. Where are they now?"

"Yes. No. It was. No idea."

"Huh." She considered this as they moved toward the next reinforced door. "Where is everyone?"

"Ordered to remain out of sight. Banished are to be considered among the dead and treated thus. The land of the dead is a barren landscape, devoid of the living. The two worlds never cross. Mine is an exceptional circumstance."

"I'd argue against the 'never cross' part," Ana murmured. "But, yeah, I think I get it. So, the villagers we met before..."

"Caught off-guard, I suppose. If they knew it was me coming to their dock, they likely would have disappeared, too. Except for the temple priestess."

"The convener for the two worlds."

Magnus smiled as he turned to look at her before passing through the next reinforced door. "Were you Barentian, you'd have been given to the temple because of your ability."

"Lucky for both of us, I'm not."

Ana's heart panged when Magnus' smile left.

"I suppose it is. Otherwise, neither of us would be here now."

They approached the final heavy door that would lead them inside. Her gaze traveled up the face of the fortress nestled into the foot of the mountain.

It was no wonder the Barentians were an unconquered people.

She caught sight of a young Barentian with the same wild hair that Magnus had, peering down at them from a gap in the rock that she guessed was a balcony or large window of some kind.

His son?

Or just another curious youth, defying the rules?

Inside, the reception hall was cavernous, but they continued past it. Magnus led Ana down a stone-lined corridor to another room that showed the first hints of warmth.

It looked like a small clerks' office, with a large desk and a wall of fitted shelves supporting scrolls, books and other miscellany that Ana itched to explore. A lit fireplace provided heat.

Electric lighting suspended above the main desk and other work benches illuminated documents and manuscripts strewn across their surfaces.

A stout woman with graying auburn hair, carrying a heavy leather-bound book, approached from a doorway tucked into the back of the room. She stopped on the opposite side of the large desk, placing the open volume with care on its surface.

There were pens and pencils of varying types and inks. The woman ignored those in favor of a quill and inkwell that she withdrew from somewhere behind the desk. She set them near the book and adjusted her glasses.

"Registrar Maerie Gailensdotter," Magnus greeted her.

Peering over the top rim of her lenses at Magnus and Ana, nose twitching as she scented them, she spoke in English. "Prince Magnus Bjornson, I presume we are recording a union. Are there any offspring to account for?"

"Shouldn't the clan shaman be here to witness the record?"

"He will not be."

Magnus grunted. "I thought my father—the king," he corrected himself, "was determined to uphold all the values and traditions that Barentia has observed for centuries?"

"Millenia," the woman corrected. "It would seem our esteemed king is allowing some changes to our traditions."

"I'm standing here, a banished man, because he refused to change anything," Magnus ground through his teeth.

The woman's gaze flicked to the open door behind them before she removed her glasses, set them next to the open inkwell, and strode toward the door. With a quick peek into the hall, she closed it and returned to her post.

Retrieving the glasses, she tapped them against her palm, regarding Magnus across the desk, then turned her inspection on Ana, nose twitching again.

The woman's frustrated indecision rippled through Ana. A psychic wasn't needed to see the unspoken words in her expression.

Magnus had made it clear that he was banished and expected to be treated as a dead man. This ritual of their impending *marriage* was the only excuse that would grant them entry into the realm.

"You are not a bear, or a shifter." Her demeanor steeled when she turned her attention to Ana.

"I am not," Ana said.

To Magnus, the registrar said, "You were serious when you said Barentia should make alliances with outsiders."

Magnus nodded.

"The king seems to have changed his mind on the subject. Outsiders come and go as freely as Barentians these days." Her gaze flicked to the door again.

The woman's growing conflicted concern weighed on Ana's senses. She wanted to tell Magnus something.

But Magnus was a banished outcast. No one was supposed to be talking to him. Her sole role here was to record his impending marriage and any offspring.

After having observed the two for the last few minutes, Ana acted on instinct. Reaching for Magnus' hand, she looked up at him and thought of their night together. The memory of his tenderness and consideration radiated through her. She smiled, allowing her growing feelings toward this gentle man to show on her face and in the way she leaned into his arm. Her thumb stroked his.

"I'm honored to have the chance to be here, in Barentia. To see your childhood home, even if just a little bit." She laughed. "Perhaps if we have many children together, I may get to see a little more of it each time. Though it would be a shame that they might not know it as you do—did."

Magnus' fingers squeezed around hers affectionately as he looked down into her face.

She sensed his emotions flipping, but the corner of his lips lifted. "*Many* children," he repeated gruffly as his gaze turned heated.

Warmth bloomed in her cheeks, spread through her chest and down her belly, at the look in his eyes.

The registrar cleared her throat.

Her expression softened as she looked between the two, appreciating their affection for one another.

"You're only supposed to be here long enough to declare for the record, but if you like, I can give you a peek at the library where Magnus spent so much time as a boy," she said to Ana, tipping her head back toward the open door she'd come through with the book.

"Maerie's duties as registrar are just part of her role here in the stronghold. She's also the clan archivist and librarian."

"And clerk and secretary," she added, proud. She reached for the quill, dipping it into the inkpot. "Shall we?"

Magnus' fingers tightened on Ana's again. She glanced up into his face. Concern creased his brow as he stared down at the book. His apprehension was palpable.

She understood.

Returning her attention to the book, she considered the elegant script lining the pages of the thick tome.

Their names were to be inscribed in the clan's official register, tracking royal lineages.

Magnus was a prince. A shaman was supposed to witness this record. This act was part of the clan's long, long tradition and should not be treated lightly.

They were there under the guise of a pending marriage. A sham. A ruse.

A lie.

Ana's chest tightened as she looked up into Magnus' conflicted face under the weight of the moment.

When he turned his gaze to her, the feeling flowing from him took her breath away.

"Analiese, before we sign this register, if you have any doubts, we can turn back now. Leave the page blank."

They were already inside the stronghold at the heart of Barentia.

They didn't have to commit to the lie to fulfill their mission. They'd just needed access to the stronghold and territory. And they had it.

But, they still needed to confirm Barentian contact with the sigil to understand what happened to Aksel.

Here, now, can we still get that information without signing the book?

Studying the script, some part of her *wanted* to sign it.

"We can turn back now if that's what *you* want. I'll understand. The past hasn't been kind to either of us."

It hadn't.

Magnus' politically contracted wife had turned against him. Ulla had alienated him from his son, his father, and his clan.

Ana had been rejected by the man she'd thought was the love of her life. Although she and Antony had been together for many years, he'd never talked of their future together. They'd been little more than friends sharing a bed until she'd lost him to the ocean. Maybe he had always known his fate was with the sea.

After she'd lost her mother and Gran and then Antony, Ana had been alone, except for her growing family at the GPSA.

Magnus had also been alone, with the exception of those that worked for the Organization—the parent of the GPSA.

We understand each other.

When Magnus touched her, she wanted him to *always* be touching her.

She'd never experienced this level of connection with anyone before. Not even Antony.

Did Magnus feel it too? Or was she just becoming infatuated with the big, stoic polar bear shifter?

After all, how long had they known each other? A week? Less?

Does it matter?

She'd experienced so much in the last year, seen so much—too much.

When she looked into Magnus' eyes, she *knew* it was the same for him.

Could either of them ever truly have a 'normal' life? Even after they closed this case?

If they closed this case.

Ana didn't think she could. She didn't even know what a 'normal' life even meant anymore.

But she did know something. Now. She looked up into Magnus' eyes.

Her heart pounded in her chest, blood roaring through her. Tears sprang to her eyes as she realized, truly, that she wanted this man.

If they were to commit their names to that precious book on the Registrar's desk, she didn't want it to be a lie.

It shouldn't be.

She blinked away the threatening tears and tried to offer an encouraging smile that told him he didn't need to sign the book.

The registrar forgotten; Ana stood transfixed as Magnus' large hand reached for her cheek. Her eyes fell closed at the feel of his warm fingers caressing her jaw to cradle her nape. His lips brushed hers.

He kissed the corner of her mouth, her cheek and his warm breath tickled her ear as he whispered, "I would sign that book in a heartbeat, if it meant that your name was recorded next to mine for all of Barentian time."

Her breath hitched as she leaned her cheek into his palm, relishing the feel of his skin on hers.

The frantic pounding of her heart slowed to a steady thrum.

When she opened her eyes, he was still bent close, his gaze searching hers.

"I would take you as my mate, should you choose it."

Mate.

Intuition roared through Ana's being. "I choose you," she said, voice steady. She returned his kiss.

"I promised to keep you safe and warm," he murmured against her lips.

"So you did," she murmured back with a smile.

A promise.

Mate.

For all Barentian time.

Maerie cleared her throat. "My ink pot is drying out."

Ana and Magnus returned their attention to the woman with the wry smile and the task at hand.

Magnus reached for the quill and, with a few swipes, set his name to the register, then held the pen up for Ana.

She plucked it from his fingers and approached the hand-crafted book. His signature was bold and elegant.

> Magnus, son of Bjorn, son of Thorn. Prince of
> Barentia.

Analiese carefully set her name next to his.

Analiese Maria Marguerita Francesca Ortega.

SIXTEEN

Magnus smiled as he stepped into the library. "This was one of my favorite places," he said to Ana.

His smile widened, noting her awe as she stared at the long room with its stacked concourses of floor to ceiling bookshelves.

Sometimes, when he was in Ireland, he'd visit the Trinity College library to soothe his homesickness. It was almost as magnificent as this one. He suspected that some rare, prestigious visitor had modeled it after the legend of the Great Library of Barentia, which was older than anyone could remember. He was sure he'd once seen cuneiform tablets stowed away in the special collections room.

He was pleased to see the oil lamps and wall sconces had been replaced with much safer electric lighting since he was last here.

If there was electricity in the stronghold, that meant there were infrastructural changes elsewhere in the territory.

I'll have to check for cell service once we're back outside.

Though he seriously doubted they would have gone so far as to erect a cell tower on the mountain. Then again, there was electricity in the place *now*.

He indulged in his appreciation of the large room's aesthetic while he observed Ana's reactions to his home.

His gaze fell to Maerie, who stood nearby, her attention on him.

"It may be blasphemous to allow you in here, and even more so to say it, but I am pleased to see you in your beloved home again, Magnus. I know what it meant to you as a boy," she said, no longer guarding herself against him.

She never had, here.

Few ever visited the beautiful repository.

After his mother's death, he'd sought sanctuary in the library when he missed her.

Maerie had recognized this in him, as she'd known it in his mother.

She was risking punishment by allowing his access to the stronghold to be prolonged longer than the signing of the register.

"He comes here too," she said, her voice quiet in the large space.

Elias.

His father Bjorn never, ever, set foot in this wing that had been dominated by his mother's presence. Servants brought anything Bjorn wanted to his rooms.

Maerie had dared another risk, to speak of the family to a banished.

Frozen, he stared at her, wanting her to say more, yet not wanting to be tempted by what she could say. He glanced up into the stacks, lest someone should be watching, listening.

Registering his apprehension, Maerie stepped closer and kept her voice low. "He is so much like you—as you were at his age. And just as lonely."

Regret tore at his heart.

Magnus nodded, acknowledging the kindness of the insight she offered him about his son. Turning his attention to the stacks, his jaw worked as he considered the unexpected onslaught of emotion, touching the leather-bound spines to ground himself.

Back under control, he returned his gaze to her patient face.

Maerie had always been kind to him, even before his mother's death. There was no doubt she'd extend the same kindness to Elias.

"He is well?"

"As healthy as can be, despite his limited freedom."

"Limited?"

Maerie nodded. "Everyone is limited. Even the young prince—especially the young prince."

Magnus frowned. A prince should expect total freedom of the realm. How else was he to know his lands and people? "He doesn't leave the stronghold?"

She shook her head. "Nor does the king. He's rarely seen."

"He's ill?"

Maerie shrugged, but kept her voice low as she answered. "No one knows. Anyone that requests his presence is redirected to Mistress Ulla. Anyone that tries to circumvent her authority is met with the king's personal guard and either turned away or imprisoned, if they're too persistent."

"What is going on here?" The sharp demand drew everyone's attention to the open door between the library and the Registrar's office.

Magnus straightened when he sighted the guard.

Havard.

Magnus' cousin, boyhood friend, and head of security.

"The Registrar was just reminding me that I am forbidden to be in here, and demanded that I leave."

Havard nodded, eyes leveled on Magnus, expression unreadable.

There was no sense of their boyhood bond or fondness in the man as Magnus approached and passed through the door, then the registrar's office, and out into the open corridor.

Ana followed close behind. Maerie lingered at the threshold of her domain.

Several more guards waited.

They expect a confrontation.

Magnus decided it was time to push inward. "I demand to see my father."

Havard tilted his head up to meet Magnus' direct gaze. "You no longer have a father."

With his head up, Havard's beard was also lifted, exposing the black mark on his throat.

Magnus' gut tightened as he stepped forward, towering over him. The other guards tensed.

Were they all marked? The Barentian's propensity toward full beards obscured their throats.

He stared Havard in the face for a long moment. Ana hovered at his periphery with their backpacks in hand.

Although his stance was one of intimidation, he hesitated out of concern for Ana's safety.

"Doesn't he have a right to see his father once more?" Ana asked Havard.

"He is banished and has no rights at all," he spat.

"Blood is still blood," Magnus said.

Something flickered in Havard's eyes, but it was so brief, Magnus wasn't sure as they continued to stare at one another.

It was something Havard would often say to Magnus in their youth.

Havard scowled. To the men, he said, "Escort them out."

One of the men grabbed Ana's arm, shoving her toward the exit so hard she stumbled into the wall, dropping their bags.

"Don't touch her," Magnus snarled at the guard. He bent to help her to her feet and retrieve the packs. When he turned back to the guards, they'd all moved into defensive positions in the narrow space.

He stepped toward the men, ensuring Ana was behind him. He looked each man in the face then said, "if any of you touch my mate again, I will rip your fucking arms off."

"Looking for a fight, Magnus?" Havard smirked. "Come on, shift."

Magnus' growl reverberated off of the stone walls and floor of the corridor as he dipped into a loose crouch, both shielding Ana and preparing to launch himself forward should he need to.

The other Barentians growled back, gripping their weapons tighter.

The stink of their fear as they faced him stained his nostrils.

A figure appeared at the end of the hall behind the guards.

Magnus' heart stumbled.

"Stop!" A high voice cut across the deafening growls.

The others stopped immediately.

Magnus let his bass growl roll out, giving himself a few extra seconds to compose his reaction to the appearance of his son.

Still fully aware of Ana's rapid breathing behind him, he didn't ease his stance.

Elias strode forward.

The multiple guards surrounding Magnus hadn't phased his heart rate.

The approach of his son sent it into a wild staccato.

Ana's small hand slipped into his palm, soothing him.

By the time Elias stood just beyond the wall of Barentian guards, Magnus had eased his posture and controlled his emotions.

Despite her gesture to calm him, her fingers trembled within his grasp and her breath remained shallow.

Elias moved between the guards.

"Your Highness—" Havard stepped between Magnus and the boy.

No, not quite a boy, or not for much longer, anyway.

Elias' throat was unmarred.

With some relief, Magnus drank in his son's features.

Hair the same as his own. He stood at a level height with Havard. He would be as tall as Magnus, if not taller.

There was little of Ulla in Elias—physically, at least.

Gods, I hope he doesn't favor her in character. My heart would truly break.

The odds were much higher, with his absence.

After a long moment, Elias turned to Havard. "I would speak with my father in the library."

"Sire, it is forbidden—."

"I *will* speak to my father," Elias spoke over Havard, making his command clear.

Magnus struggled to maintain his impassive expression.

Did Elias remember him? He hadn't thought he would, since he was so young when Magnus left.

No, more likely that he'd heard Magnus had returned for the signing and was curious.

Elias strode through the Registrar's office, acknowledging her with a dip of his head. "Madam Gailensdotter."

Movement drew Magnus' attention to the far end of the hall that connected to a cross corridor where Elias had come from. Several figures hovered and ducked behind the corners.

Ignoring Havard, Magnus pressed Ana's fingers, pulling her ahead of himself to follow Elias back into the library.

As much as he'd dreamed of seeing Elias again, he never thought it would happen.

Magnus wasn't sure if he was ready for this.

He released her hand so that she wouldn't detect the tremble that shook his own hands now.

SHOCK, DELIGHT, AND FEAR swept through Ana on seeing Elias.

That was all layered on the instinctive terror that had ripped through her when the snarling echo-chamber had engulfed her senses.

She was so wide open, trying to read every little bit she could, anything that might help Magnus in some way.

The guards' fear of Magnus assaulted her.

Magnus' refusal to back down shored up her courage.

Even the librarian's distress over the confrontation was palpable.

And just like that, a single word cut through it all, allowing her a reprieve to draw breath against the powerful emotions stifling her.

Elias.

The tenor of the atmosphere changed so rapidly it jolted her off balance.

Sandwiched between the young prince and Magnus as they went back to the library, she struggled to control the flow of emotional energy surrounding her—against their conflicted emotions surging against one another like waves trapped in a pool.

In the library, Elias and Magnus took each other's measure.

Ana took theirs.

Elias: *You're here. You left me. You shouldn't be here. I can't believe you're here. We don't have much time. Take me with you.*

Magnus: *My boy. I miss you. You've grown. I never thought I'd see you again. We don't have much time. I need to get you away from here.*

"We don't have much time," Ana blurted, latching on to the most obvious. "Analiese Ortega," she said, shoving her hand toward the prince.

The corner of his lips quirked—like Magnus' did—before he accepted her proffered hand and shook it. "Elias Magnusson."

"Should I curtsy?" she whispered to Magnus.

Elias laughed, releasing some of the tension in his broad shoulders.

Ana glanced toward the door where the guards hovered, scowling.

The registrar remained at the threshold of the doorway, hands clasped so hard her knuckles were white.

"You don't have much time," Ana reminded them and moved away to give them a sense of privacy as she put her backpack on.

"No, we don't. The guards will have gone to fetch my mother," Elias said, scorn lacing his voice. "She forbade me from seeing you when the messenger announced your arrival at the village."

"Yet here you are," Magnus said.

Elias dipped his head, looking like the youth that he actually was.

Ana's heart swelled as their sense of longing overwhelmed her. Their desire to embrace for the first time in a decade.

Oh God, please hug each other before I crumble.

Before someone comes to pull you apart again.

It was all they wanted. That, and to leave Barentia.

She ground her teeth as they continued to face one another, neither reaching for the other.

Footsteps echoing in the stone corridor filtered in through the open door.

Damn it!

Just hug, damn it!

She desperately wanted to shove them together or blurt out what each was feeling to the other as they stubbornly remained silent.

The footsteps were louder now.

Her fingers dug into the straps of Magnus' pack gripped in her hands.

"I'm glad to see you again," Elias said to Magnus.

"As am I," Magnus smiled at his son, letting all his barriers melt away. A true, open smile.

The footsteps stopped. "Elias, I forbade you from coming here today," the woman's voice snapped through the room.

Elias stiffened.

Magnus' smile disappeared before he slowly turned around to face her.

"Ulla."

Ana looked from Magnus to Ulla's barely suppressed triumphant expression.

Her heart dropped.

This can't be good.

Her gaze met the apology in Magnus' eyes.

She slowly closed her eyes, resolved, and returned his gaze.

I trust you.

His face tightened, but he locked his feelings down before they gave him away.

Regret.

"Elias, you are to remain in your room until I decide your punishment," Ulla's hard voice made the boy flinch.

He said nothing to his mother.

His expression full of longing as he spared Magnus a last glance, he strode out of the library through the main door at the far end, rather than squeeze through everyone gathered here.

Poor kid.

Ulla ignored Ana, walking up to Magnus. "The banished are forbidden to speak to anyone in Barentia without official cause. Especially the royal family. I charge you with treason for attempting to influence the true heir of the realm."

Satisfaction roiled off of her like a heavy perfume.

Ana's fingers curled into a fist, as she wanted nothing more than to punch the woman in the face. Twice. No, twice wasn't even enough.

Ulla had used the prince to entrap Magnus.

Of course, Elias would defy her order to see his long-lost father. Possibly a once in a lifetime chance. What youth wouldn't rebel against an order like that?

They'd both expected it—Elias and Magnus. Both accepted the risks.

Did Elias understand the magnitude of the risk for Magnus?

Ana didn't think so.

"Lock these two up separately until I decide what to do with them," Ulla said to the guards and walked out.

Rage ripped through Ana. She shook with it. Struggled to control it.

It wasn't Magnus' feelings.

They were her own.

She'd never ever felt that about anyone in her life before.

How dare this piece of shit be so cavalier?

A guard reached for her.

Magnus snarled at the guard, then shoved him so hard he bounced off the stone wall with a crack. "Leave, Ana; take the plane and go home."

She was shaking her head before the words came. "No."

"Havard is marked. Like Aksel. Come back with Kane and the others."

Rooted to the stone floor, her gaze swept the scene before her. Magnus blocked the guards' access to her. She had a clear path out if she could remember the way.

"If you don't, they may kill both of us."

Would they?

Still, she remained frozen for what seemed minutes when, in reality, it was mere seconds.

She stepped toward Magnus and he roared in her face, allowing his features to morph into the fierce polar bear he was, sending shocks of terror through her nervous system.

She was running before she knew she was moving as she passed through the door to the first courtyard.

Kane.

She had to let Kane know they had confirmation that other Barentians were marked.

Kane would get Magnus out.

The Organization wouldn't abandon one of their own. Ana didn't know Aaron Connor very well, but she knew Raya Burns enough to know that she'd never leave Magnus to rot in a Barentian dungeon. And where Raya went, so went Ian, her formidable mate.

And Carson. She had no idea what his relationship to Magnus was, but Ana knew he'd help her, as would Lirikai.

She clung to the absolute knowledge that she wouldn't be alone. If she could get to the plane. A plane she didn't know how to fly, but that wouldn't stop her from trying.

Magnus, the banished, was still inside the stronghold. Everywhere outside of the stronghold remained deserted.

She passed through the curtain wall and across the last sheltered space toward the final exit, not daring to look back at how close any pursuers were. Her hammering heart, whooshing breath, the swish of her pumping arms and frantic boot falls made hearing anything other than herself impossible.

Belatedly, she realized she'd dropped Magnus' pack at some point, as her own bounced on her back. She ran harder, putting as much distance between herself and the stronghold as she could.

Her initial terror-fueled jump-start was fading as regular adrenaline rushed her veins.

It was a long, long way back to the village where they had docked their little seaplane.

As her muscles strained, she finally spared a glance over her shoulder. If anyone were pursuing her, surely they'd have caught her by now. They were shifters with far more strength and speed than any human.

The expanse of road between herself and the stronghold was empty.

Why hadn't they stopped her? Ulla had said to detain both of them.

Was she just not important enough to waste their time?

God, I hope so.

She never wanted to be so unimportant in her life.

Ana kept going as she considered her options, should someone try to stop her. She had her gun and her taser. Her pack held some few supplies, but not much.

SEVENTEEN

THE SUN WAS STILL below the horizon by the time the dark outlines of the fishing village came into sight in the dim light.

Her fatigued muscles threatened to drag her down into the snow.

How long had she been running?

The road declined sharply toward the village, forcing her to move with more care.

Would the villagers stop her? Had word somehow been sent that she'd escape the stronghold?

Magnus wasn't with her. Surely, they'd be suspicious, considering they were there to record their impending union. Banished, Magnus was forbidden to stay.

A distant sound drew her attention. Standing motionless, straining to determine what it was.

It was the whine of engines. Boats?

She hurried down through the village path.

This time, there was no one to witness her arrival. It was dark and silent. Eerily silent. Like the village was abandoned.

She rounded the downward bend, eyes searching the small harbor for their plane.

The dock was empty.

No! No, no, no!

She slipped the rest of the way down the path, desperately scanning the ocean in case maybe the tether had come untied and it drifted nearby.

The whine of engines grew louder, but there were no boats visible on the horizon.

The sound came from behind her.

Moments later, snowmobiles came into view.

Is there any other way off this island?

Even if there was somewhere to swim to, she'd freeze in the Barents Sea at this time of year—*any* time of year, if she were honest.

She considered drawing her gun. Instead, she ran back up the path, frantically tugging the doors to some houses.

All locked.

The snowmobiles were deafeningly close.

The temple. She darted toward the divine sanctuary. Locked.

She stared at it in disbelief.

Who locks temple doors?

Anyone trying to keep riffraff out.

Spinning around, she scanned the darkness, searching for somewhere to hide, then crouched, moving through the shadows.

Grunting against the strain in her exhausted muscles, she broke for the forest. Maybe there was some other way off the island.

There has to be a boat somewhere, right?

At the edge of the village, she gauged the distance between the cover of the buildings and the forest's edge above it. The snow cover was pristine, with little hint of how deep it was or how uneven the ground was beneath it.

She'd leave a glaring trail.

Her gut told her they weren't a surprise rescue crew sent by Kane. They would have identified themselves.

Run. Hide. Run. Hide.

Heart pounding, she ducked back as a black-clad snowmobiler sped past her hidden position.

They were circling, no doubt searching for her.

Unless, coincidentally, someone else was on the run from the Barentian authorities?

She huffed.

Where the hell is everyone?

Were they hiding inside, or had they all left?

"What are you going to do, Ana?" she muttered, watching for the next passing snowmobile.

Who are these people? Barentians?

Why aren't they just sniffing her out?

Because they aren't Barentian? They're probably the humans that the priestess mentioned.

The darkness.

Think Ana.

Another whizzed past her position.

She grit her teeth, trying to focus while hiding in an abandoned village from the deafening whine of snowmobile engines after running for what seemed an eternity.

Deep breath. Listen.

All she could hear was the incessant whining of the snowmobiles and the drum of her heart in her ears.

She crept along the wall to peer between the houses. The searchers were running their vehicles along the narrow paths.

She ducked back, flat against the wall.

You can keep trying to get into a building or make a run for the forest. Maybe there's another village along the coast with a boat.

Steal a snowmobile?

I'm trapped if I don't.

Ana, you don't know how to drive a snowmobile any more than you know how to fly a plane!

Hide. Run. Hijack.

Fan-freaking-tastic.

Reaching for her taser, her fingers closed around it.

Next one.

She crouched and scuttled closer to the edge of the building where she hid, waiting for the next pass.

With my luck, I'd tase one, Buddy would fly off and the damned thing would crash.

How to get one to stop?

Maybe let one see her?

God, I can't think straight!

She spared the open space toward the forest another glance. The snow was no longer pristine, as it was now marred with tracks from her pursuers.

A whining shadow raced toward her position.

The second it passed her, she launched forward, racing for the forest's edge. She dashed across the vehicle's tracks, and scrambled to climb the rocky incline to reach the darkness below the evergreens.

The noise behind her continued.

The trees were just yards away.

Pain pierced her back, instantly followed by the sharp snap of electricity jolting her body.

Fuck.

Rigid, she was dimly aware of falling back down the rock face toward a dark figure with an extended arm.

She wasn't the only one with a taser.

MAGNUS WOKE TO CHAINS dragging his wrists and ankles toward the stone floor.

Ana.

Was she safe? Did she make it to the plane?

Head pounding, he groaned as he struggled to sit upright, sliding his back along the rough wall.

The damp scents of barely frozen earth told him he was in the dungeon, while the shackles growled of an impossible escape.

Cracking an eye open, he confirmed his location with the sight of the banded oak door at the far end of the narrow cell, thanks to the illumination of an electric light affixed to the ceiling.

Fuck.

Escape would be impossible so long as he sported these chains. They made them to hold powerful shifters—like polar bear shifters. None had ever failed. Even against his bloodline. The biggest and strongest of Barentians. The reason they were the chosen kings in the days when they were under constant threat of warfare from neighboring territories.

At least he'd given Ana enough time to get out of the stronghold while he'd blocked anyone from immediately chasing her down.

With any luck, she'd be on the plane and on her way to meet with Kane.

He swallowed against the sudden dryness in his mouth.

Or, they caught her, and she's in the cell next door.

He had no way of knowing either.

If he'd ignored the temptation to speak to his son, Ana would be safe.

She trusted me to keep her safe.

They'd be on their way off this island together if he'd just adhered to the law.

She's an agent, Magnus. You were both here on a mission.

And what did they gain?

Confirmation that things weren't right here? Likely nothing to do with their mission, just clan politics.

That at least one other Barentian, on Barentian soil, bore a sigil.

Havard. Head of his father's guard.

Neither Elias nor Ulla were marked.

So, what does this mean?

He held his wrists up, shook his head, and dropped them again. The chain dragged and rattled against the flagstone floor with his movement.

"Well, Magnus, looks like you've got all the time in the world to figure it out now."

Was he down here to rot? Or simmer?

Ulla had charged him with treason. His father would have the final say on that, and his punishment.

They had already banished him.

That left life in prison or execution. They weren't likely to send him on his merry way.

He glanced up at the glaring light source.

His father had refused any type of infrastructural changes to the territory for decades.

Why now, in the time of Magnus' absence? After years of trying to convince him Barentia should modernize with the rest of the world?

Ulla.

Maybe his father had been right. The changes since he'd been gone didn't seem to benefit those few that he'd encountered since his arrival, despite the convenience of lighting up the dark spaces that traditionally were lit by oil lamps or torch.

There hadn't been any power lines or solar panels attached to the houses in the fishing village.

Were any of the island's other villages the same?

It would be out of character for his father to actually implement something on the island and not extend it to the benefit of the rest of Barentia.

Whereas, Ulla never gave a shit about anyone other than Ulla.

Not even Elias.

So, what is going on?

Magnus swallowed hard as a sudden wave of despair washed over him.

Surely my father isn't marked like Havard,

Impossible.

Bjorn Thornsson could be led by a pretty face, but he'd never be one's whelp. Never.

Doubt continued to scratch at Magnus' nape.

There was nothing he could do until someone opened the door.

⸻

ULLA MATOCHKIN PACED THE expanse of her private suite within the stronghold, chewing the edge of her left thumbnail.

Her right hand vibrated from the incoming message on her cell phone.

With a quick glance at the message, her lips stretched into a triumphant grin.

It had taken an awful lot of conniving to get satellite Internet in place to provide Wi-Fi to the archaic island. A *lot* of conniving, but it was already paying off.

"Gotcha."

Tucking the device into her pocket, she strode toward the door and made her way down to the dungeons.

I finally have Magnus by the balls.

Now it's time to twist.

Descending the stone steps with a light skip, Ulla ignored the baleful look of the lockmaster as she breezed toward him.

He unlocked the cell door and swung it open on silent hinges in time for her to step through without a break in her stride.

These Barentians are so well trained. Everyone in their place, fulfilling their roles to perfection.

She stepped into the cell.

Except Magnus.

He looked directly at her from his seated position on the stone floor, wrists and ankles encased in heavy Barentian manacles, expression guarded.

Many of her own people had fallen to the weight of those manacles in the long past.

Forearms resting on drawn-up knees, he laced his fingers together. The only signal of his agitation. "Ulla."

"Regent. You may call me Regent now."

That had him on his feet. "What's wrong with my father?"

"You have no father, *banished*."

His steel-gray eyes glinted as his jaw tightened. "He still has the final word on my fate, Ulla. Regent or not."

"Maybe," she said with a shrug. "If he's feeling up for it. If not, I will. As I do everything else these days."

"What do you want?"

"From you? Absolutely nothing more than to see you break."

Magnus snorted.

"What's so funny?" Every muscle in her body went rigid at his affront.

Gods I hate this man.

Her eyes flicked the length of him, head to toe, unable to resist assessing his attractive physical traits. She drew a deep breath. His scent invaded her senses, triggering memories. Images of their marriage bed tumbled through her mind, dragging her into their past—the best parts of it, for a few seconds.

"You're still as petty as ever."

"Regardless of what your skewed perception of me is, you're in prison and I have the power to save your life or end it."

"What do you want from me, Ulla?" he repeated, voice dropping in his displeasure.

"What I've always wanted, Magnus. Your cooperation. That's all."

"You don't want cooperation. You want everyone to kiss your ass."

"Same thing." She smiled.

"No, it isn't. Is that why you had Havard marked with a control sigil? Because he wouldn't kiss your ass? And Aksel too? Did he finally see how corrosive you truly are? How many others?"

The smile fell from her face. "Aksel? I would never—what are you talking about? Where is he?"

Her heart pounded harder with each second as his silence stretched.

Aksel had been on the ship that was seized, overseeing its journey to its distribution port.

Her ears rang as her head swam.

He escaped with the other crew members and just hadn't reported in yet.

Her fingers slid over the cellphone in her pocket. She drew a steadying breath. Any time now, he'd message her he was in the clear and returning soon.

But how could Magnus know Aksel had been on *that* ship? How much did he know about the sigils?

"Who are your new friends, Ulla? Who have you let into Barentia?"

He's fishing for the Organization.

Is that why he was really here?

What else does he know?

"When were you supposed to get married, Magnus? Or did you drag that useless human here for nothing?"

He glared at her.

"She didn't get far," Ulla smirked.

Magnus growled, rising to his feet. "Where is she?"

"Where is Aksel?"

"He's lying unconscious, under the care of GPSA medics. Where is Ana?"

"*Care?*" She stepped toward Magnus.

"Ana."

"Picked up by some friends of mine."

Magnus' eyes narrowed as he stepped toward Ulla, growling louder, despite the pull of the chains.

She stepped back toward the door, fear rippling throughout her body.

"Are these friends the same friends that marked Aksel with a sigil and beat him so badly he had to crawl into a control room panel to escape them?"

Pain bloomed in Ulla's chest as her lungs constricted.

Polar bear shifters never, ever crawled.

And certainly not Aksel...

Not Aksel.

"He wouldn't..." Wulker wouldn't. Nor would... Not to Aksel.

"Who wouldn't what?" Magnus pressed. "Who wouldn't what, Ulla? Your friend wouldn't do that to your little brother?"

"Shut up, Magnus," she snarled back, unable to think, her gut twisted so hard.

Ulla studied her ex-husband's stony face. He'd never been a liar.

But things change. He was an agent for the Organization.

Agents lie.

But how else could he know Aksel was on that ship, or about the sigils?

She met his eyes.

Her instinct told her he was being truthful.

Aksel was in trouble. Real trouble.

"Call your agency and have him brought to Barentia."

Magnus shook his head. "He specifically didn't want that."

"You said he's unconscious." She stepped forward, hands fisted.

"He is."

"You're making no sense."

"Ana communicated with him in the astral where he's trapped in bear form."

Ulla gasped, gaze dropping to the floor as her mind raced.

Magnus went on. "He's trapped in a sea of black ink or oil, or something."

She reached for the wall as her knees buckled.

Oh Gods, no.

"You and I—and Ana—can go to where Aksel is being safeguarded and you can see him for yourself."

Why? Why would Wulker do this to Aksel?

Aksel had to have challenged him. But *why?*

What was he thinking?

"It's too late for her—your human." Ulla squared her shoulders, lifting her chin as she glared back at Magnus. "That's on you, Magnus. You brought her here."

EIGHTEEN

ANA'S HEAD SPUN BEHIND her closed lids, brain pounding.

Magnus. I have to help Magnus.

Her body ached from the tasing.

God, I feel awful. I owe Raya a colossal apology.

The spinning in her head seemed to have gathered cotton in her ears, muffling any sound around her.

Stink crept up her nostrils.

Not brisk northern air.

Where am I?

She cracked her eyes open into more darkness, then let them close again.

Her hands grazed her waist, noting that her weapons were gone. Pulling her cell from her pocket, she confirmed there was no service before she tapped the flashlight function to illuminate her surroundings.

Oh no. No, no, no.

Above her was the familiar view of the interior roof of a cargo container.

They must have drugged her to keep her unconscious, to get her into one.

She groaned, trying to roll onto her side.

"I'd lie still for a while if I were you. It'll take some time for the drugs to wear off. We don't want you puking all over the place," someone said from nearby.

"Smells like someone already did," she groaned.

"Exactly. Don't need any more of that, along with everything else." The face to the voice loomed over her, squinting from the light. He held up a water bottle. "Drink this when the spinning stops."

"Are we on a ship?" With her head already spinning, she couldn't tell.

"Not yet."

A second face, creased with concern, loomed over her.

Ana's heart stopped. She blinked as she squeaked, "Antony?"

"Antony? No, I'm Emilio. You know Antony?" the first man said.

"You can see me?" Antony asked, astonished. "It's about goddammned time, Ana!"

"What do you mean, it's about time?" she demanded. "I've been trying to reach you since you died."

"Uhm. Ma'am, maybe you should drink some water sooner rather than later." Emilio put the water on the floor next to her.

She pushed herself into a sitting position, balanced her phone on her knee, then swiped the bottle, uncapped and guzzled its contents as she glared up at Antony next to her.

"Thanks," she said to Emilio when she finished.

"Are you alright? You seemed to have hit your head. There's some blood," Emilio said, waving an index finger in a circle toward her.

She had some vague recollection of bouncing off rocks on her way down while she was being tased.

"Maybe that's why I can see you," she said to Antony.

Antony shrugged.

"Yeah, sure," Emilio said, stepping back.

Ana turned her attention to her surroundings. She swept the room with her light. She and Emilio and Antony weren't alone. A dozen other scattered people in the confines of the cargo container squinted at her with varying expressions of concern and annoyance. A few ignored her altogether.

"God, this is so bad."

"No kidding," Emilio said.

"Why are you here?" she said to Antony.

"Because you need to save them," he said, exasperated.

Emilio said, "because they picked us up after the confusion of the accident. Hey, you mentioned Antony and trying to reach him since he died. You're not Analiese, are you?"

Ana froze. "How do you know my name?" she grabbed the flashlight phone, aiming it at Emilio. He wore a dirty uniform. Shining the light back down the length of the room again, she noted several more men in uniforms. "Oh, my god," she whispered.

"Yeah, Ana. I told you to *save* them, not *join* them."

"You," she jabbed a finger in Antony's direction. "Your sarcasm isn't helping."

"I, uh..." Emilio said.

"You," she turned to Emilio. "You're one of Antony's crew mates, right? You were on his ship when the accident happened? How the hell are you *here*? And yes, I'm Antony's ... friend, Analiese."

"I should ask you that same question."

"Put the light out, will ya? You're blinding us. There's no cell service, so you might as well turn it off," one of the other captives said.

She switched it off, throwing the room back into darkness, and tucked the device into her pocket.

Ana sat in the darkness listening to her own breath and those of the other people trapped with her. Eventually, her eyes adjusted to the darkness and she could see the cracks of light outlining the door at the far end of the box.

This is real. This is real.

I'm trapped in a fucking cargo container.

I should have ignored Carson's call.

"Maybe, but that's not helping you right now," Antony said. Jolted, she gaped.

Antony can hear my thoughts.

"Yeah. I can."

Just like Aksel in his Bear form.

"Who?"

Never mind. Where the hell have you been? All this time?

"Mostly bouncing between here, keeping an eye on my boys and trying to get your attention, Ana. So much for being a psychic if you can't even hear me when I'm yelling at you."

She drew her legs up, curled her arms around her shins and rested her pounding forehead on her knees.

You were in my nightmares.

"Nightmares? I was trying to show you what happened, Ana. And that my guys needed your help! Do you know how exhausting this is?"

Sorry. It's probably the guilt. It creates a barrier sometimes.

Tears stung her eyes.

Yeah, what kind of psychic am I when you needed me most?

"Hey, don't cry, Ana."

Don't cry? This is all my fault. And if they're still here after all this time, there's nothing I can do to save them.

"This is not your fault, sweetheart. It's because of you they're even alive."

She sniffled, dabbing her eyes on her sleeve.

What do you mean?

She had the sense he'd settled next to her. His energy felt closer, stronger as it mingled with hers.

"I-uh," he sighed. "Ana, I'm sorry I pushed you away when you tried to warn me something bad was going to happen at sea. Your ability kept these guys alive. Even though *I* died, I could save them because your warnings gave me the edge I needed to react in time to get them out."

The Navy is still investigating.

"Yeah, I've been watching that, too. They're doing their best, but you need to let them know what happened."

Ana snorted.

Right.

"No really. We're going to figure out how to get you out of here," Antony insisted.

Ana laughed. Someone shuffled further away.

Antony, they've been trapped for over a month If they—trained for conflict guys—haven't been able to escape, how do you think I *can?*

"You, sweetheart, have me. Now that you're listening."

She grit her teeth.

You haven't changed.

"Why should I?"

Aren't you supposed to be all-knowing and full of compassion and grace in the afterlife?

"Yeah, sure, but I got things to do first. Like save my guys, then I can go slap some wings on my back. Help me out here."

She rubbed her temples, praying the pounding would ease soon so that she could deal with this ... what the hell was this?

"Life, Ana. This is life," Antony said, dropping some of his bluster.

A cool prickling sensation drifted across her cheek.

If there had been more light in the room, she would have seen Antony's hand caressing her face.

She leaned into it.

I really miss you.

"Me too, sweetheart."

She had the impression he pressed a staticky kiss on her forehead.

"I have an idea. Do you know how to bi-locate, like that girl that you interviewed did?"

Just in theory. I'm not skilled enough in my ability yet. Any time Maeda tried to guide me through the process, I just snapped back into my body.

"Hmm. Okay, that won't work. We'll just keep it simple then. I'll guide you through an escape."

Ana thought of Raya's prison break—how she used her Ashray ability to guide Chuck Meduse out of the prison to freedom. The other inmates had thought he was psychic or delusional.

Her cargo mates would likely come to the same conclusions about her.

"Nah, I told them you're gifted."

Yeah, I don't know about that anymore.

"Stop feeling sorry for yourself and help me help you help them."

You could let me wallow for at least ten minutes, Antony. It's been a pretty crappy few hours and my head is still swimming.

"You're still alive, I'm dead. I'll give you five minutes before we start planning."

Ana sighed.

Nope, you haven't changed at all.

MAGNUS' NEED TO FIND and protect Ana warred with his desire to crush Ulla's throat with his teeth.

He'd never wasted his time hating anyone in his life, but right now, he had nothing but time to hate Ulla. His hands curled into fists.

When they banished him, he'd lost his world.

This disconnection, this powerlessness... that was nothing compared to this.

On his feet, he paced as far as the chains would allow, which wasn't far.

Knowing Ana was in danger while he remained trapped in this cell at Ulla's command, tore at him.

He didn't care that she was clearly distraught over Aksel's current position.

That's her problem—her fault.

There was no doubt in his mind all of this was her fault.

Barentia's downfall would be on her head.

He just couldn't decide if he'd seek her out and crush her before he went after Ana, or come back and do it then.

If he ever got out.

No.

When.

When he got out.

Ulla wanted to see him break?

Fuck her.

Rage tore through him. Pain stabbed his wrists and ankles, dropping him to his knees, forcing him to control his instinctive desire to shift into his bear.

Magnus, you can't afford broken wrists and ankles. Ana needs you.

He ground his teeth against the pain, forcing his animal to calm.

On his knees, panting, sweat slicking his forehead, he stared at his partially shifted hands, claws extended. The manacles bit into the flesh of his wrist as his body strained against the cuffs.

He willed calm and control throughout his body, removing the edge that allowed his body to return to full human form.

Save that for later.

Instinct later, thought now.

How to get out?

Once out, his way to freedom wouldn't be too complex—as long as there weren't many guards, or these chains, to contend with.

Remove chains, escape cell...

Three paces one way, three paces back.

The heavy lock clicked, drawing Magnus' attention to the cell door.

The lockmaster swung it open, flanked by half a dozen guards. "It's time."

Magnus' gaze flicked over their resolute faces. As far as he could tell, none were marked, but they were all prepared to carry out their orders. No matter what.

Magnus was no longer their prince. He was banished—a prisoner of the realm.

Now isn't the time to escape. Not yet.

He nodded.

... maybe I can take Elias with me...

He buried that thought as quickly as it came and waited while the lockmaster unfastened his chains from the wall.

Magnus' mind worked as they moved through the dungeon corridors, up the winding stone steps, twisting and turning down the too familiar halls of his former home.

My son's home. Elias.

He couldn't help block the thoughts of his son from his mind. He might see him again.

My boy.

No.

Ana. Ana needs my help. Ulla's partners have her. She isn't safe.

Magnus clenched his jaw, his instinct to protect both his son and his mate conflicting and overwhelming.

Every muscle in his body tensed as he passed through the open double doors into the ancient Great Hall. The sounds of his chains echoed through the vast room with each step toward his fate.

Two guards preceded him with two behind, and two on either side. More at key positions of the expansive room, as was expected when the king held court.

Escape wouldn't be easy from here. He considered his other options as he moved forward.

At the far end, his father occupied the throne. Elias stood to the right of the throne while Ulla stood to the left.

Where is the shaman?

His father, his son, his former wife—the three people he'd committed his life to, before his banishment.

He sucked in a breath as unexpected emotions slammed through him.

Betrayal. Regret. Disgust.

He focused on Elias as he approached his father's judgment.

No matter what, he'd imprint his son's face in his memory.

Even if he, too, hated him and turned his back on Magnus.

"Stop there," Ulla commanded.

Ignoring her, he turned his attention to his father, ten paces before him.

Sadness swallowed every other emotion.

Bjorn Thornsson, King of the Barentian Polar Bear Shifters, was no longer the physically robust ruler exuding power that he'd been when Magnus last laid eyes on him.

The arm of the throne supported his shrunken, sallow form. His once thick white and gray hair hung in limp strings to either side of his hollowed cheeks and bleary eyes.

Magnus sniffed. *Not right*. His father smelled of slow rot from the inside out.

Illness?

How?

Magnus searched for a mark denoting Ulla's influence on the elder man. His high collar encased his throat below his thinned beard.

Magnus turned on Ulla, ready to throw accusations at her.

She met his gaze, but there was no triumph or delight in her eyes. Fear?

Couldn't be. What is there for Ulla to fear? Here? Now? No.

He stayed his words.

"Magnus the Banished," his father rasped, still denying Magnus his paternal surname.

Still not Magnus Bjornson in Barentia's eyes.

He sucked in a breath at the resurgence of rejection, attempting to re-bury it.

He straightened his shoulders, staring at the sick old man, willing him to get on with his judgment.

The old man's jaw worked before he spoke. "I charge you with treason for attempting to influence the true heir of the realm," Bjorn repeated Ulla's words almost verbatim, panting against the energy those words cost him.

Magnus' keen hearing picked up the subtle movements of the guards surrounding him. Clenching fists on weapons, shuffling feet, deep breaths.

They were prepared for him to resist. To fight.

They expected it.

Gladly. But not yet.

Not yet.

Magnus kept his features neutral as he leveled his gaze at Elias' drawn expression.

"In consideration of your previous position as heir and member of the ruling family, I shall grant you mercy."

Tears glazed Elias' eyes.

Magnus nodded.

Execution then.

"By rights of the condemned, I claim my entitlement to a final interview with the clan shaman."

"You do not observe the clan ways," Ulla blurted.

"Hm," Magnus grunted, looking at his ex-wife. "Perhaps in my last moments, I'll make my final statements. One of which *may* indicate which facility Aksel is in, where they're working to keep him alive."

"You bast—."

"Tradition dictates that I have three days before the allotted execution date, doesn't it? Plenty of confinement time to consider my last words."

Ulla's fingers curled into fists as she struggled to control herself.

"Three days. The sooner you bring the shaman to me, the sooner I may relieve my conscience and set my soul right. So that I might not haunt my executioners."

Bjorn's glassy eyes found Magnus' face, frowning as he regarded him.

Magnus couldn't read him. He never could.

What happened to this family?

What has Ulla been filling his head with, all this time?

Before her arrival at Barentia, Magnus' relationship with his father wasn't exactly loving, but it was mutually respectful and healthy despite their differences of opinion on certain matters.

Ulla had always wanted control. She had it. In his absence, she'd gained control as regent, bridging the rulership between his still-living father and too-young son.

She was threatened by Magnus' appearance to sign the register, recording his impending union.

Insecure in her position?

"Summon the clan shaman," Bjorn wheezed, then waved Magnus away.

The guards' expressions were uncertain as they exchanged glances before they moved to fulfill their order.

Magnus looked at Elias one last time. "You will be a fine king someday."

He turned and left the Great Hall his ancestors had ruled for centuries. Probably for the last time.

Three days.

Magnus had three days to figure out an escape, or he'd fail Ana, Elias, and Barentia.

NINETEEN

CLANGING AND BANGING PRECEDED the opening of the cargo box door. Everyone squinted against the sudden splash of light filling the room.

"Breakfast," Antony said.

Two goons stood on either side of the door, holding automatic rifles, while two more distributed food.

Emilio shoved a bowl of gruel with a chunk of bread into Ana's hands. "Yummy," she muttered, staring at the gray slop.

The pounding and spinning in her head had gone away after a few hours of sleep, making it easier to focus and think.

Emilio and the other crew members settled around Ana before the doors closed, throwing them back into darkness.

She'd heard them whispering among themselves whenever she was awake, catching snippets here and there.

"What do you want to know?" she said, raising the spoon, hoping it was high enough to reach her mouth in the dark. After a few seconds, she lifted the bowl to her chin and just shoveled it in, gagged once, and powered on. She hadn't eaten since the snacks she and Magnus had consumed on their way to the stronghold.

"Antony."

"Okay."

"He said you're gifted. Like, woo-woo gifted."

Ana struggled against snorting the gruel out through her nose. "I guess you could call it that."

Did you seriously describe me as 'woo-woo' gifted to them, Antony?

"It was the only way to get them to understand what I was talking about when I tried to be polite about it."

"We figured he didn't make it after he got us out. He was, uhm... right in the middle of the, uhm... blast," Emilio said, then sucked in a breath.

"No. He didn't," she said, her voice soft. "The navy is going on the assumption none of you made it since they didn't recover you. Dead or alive."

"So they're not even looking for us," one of the other guys said.

"They're investigating. That's all I know," Ana said.

"No one in the world knows we're here," another said.

"No one knows any of us are here," a woman said from further away.

"No, but that doesn't mean no one's looking," Ana said. "It's what I do. I'm part of a team investigating this group that's stealing people, and selling them."

"That's fucking awesome," the woman said, laughing. "And you're in here with us."

"Yeah, thanks for pointing out the obvious. That's what Antony said, too."

"What? He's here with us? You weren't just crazed from that bump on your head?"

"Nah, I'm always crazed, bump or not. And yes, Antony is here. He's been here with you all this time and apparently trying to tell me about it. But I've had... communication issues."

Emilio grunted.

"My crew will come looking for us. We were so close. They'll find us," she said with more uplift in her voice than she felt in her gut.

"Yeah, how are they going to do that? We don't even know where the hell we are," the woman snapped.

"Well, they grabbed me from an island nation in the middle of the Barents Sea, so I expect we're still in that region or very close. My team knew where I was. And now that I've gone missing, they'll hone in."

"Lady, it takes a lot to find boats in vast areas like that."

"I'm aware. My crew is... special," she said, thinking of Carson's ability to shift into a water dragon. Ian too. Lirikai was also a fierce aquatic hunter. Raya was a hell of a fighter and could go anywhere there was a water source.

And Magnus. He'd be magnificent as his polar bear self. Her chest tightened, thinking of him. Had he broken free from the guards? Did Kane go in after him, guns blazing—or whatever it was she did?

"Like Navy Seals or SAS?"

"Yeah, something like that, but... more. A lot more."

"Bullshit," someone scoffed.

"Listen, Ana," Emilio spoke. "If Antony is here, can you tell him thank you for keeping us alive? Even if we got picked up by these pricks."

"Tell them they're all welcome and that wasn't part of the plan."

Emilio laughed when Ana relayed his words. "No shit, huh?"

"Have you all been together this whole time?"

"Our crew? Yeah, for the most part. We don't even know who these pricks are or what they want from us, but we've seen a lot of other folks coming and going. I think we're here because we're the troublemakers," he gave a short laugh.

"They're traffickers. Everything from drugs, weapons, animals, people—anything their clients want."

"Animals? Yeah, that makes sense. A while back, they had us in another crate and something happened that made the guards panic and all we could hear was roaring. Like a lion or something. Made all the hair on my body stand on end; kinda glad we were locked in here."

"It *was* a polar bear. Pretty freaky seeing it going wild like that before they brought it down with a tranq. I went to see what all the noise was when the roaring started," Antony said.

"A polar bear?" Ana asked. Aksel?

"Who knows?" Emilio said.

Antony said, "Yeah, big son of a bitch, too. It was weird. That girl you talked to that split?"

"Bi-located? Sascha?"

"Yeah, the one that gave you my message. She was there. I thought maybe the animal had tried to attack her or something because it went nuts when they pulled her out of the box. Emilio and the guys had stepped in and tried to protect her from some nasty shit they were doing to her a few days before. I thought they were going to feed her to it or something."

"Sascha? You've seen her?" the woman asked.

"Yes. My team seized the ship she was on. Everyone on board was rescued."

The woman sobbed. "Oh, thank God. Thank God. She's my student. I teach her English. They grabbed us together while on holiday. I'm so glad she made it out."

"Yeah, we were all worried the creepy guy got her," Emilio said.

"Creepy guy?"

"There's two of 'em in charge," Antony said.

"Who are they?" Ana asked.

"A guard mentioned Wulker," a crewman said.

"Adolf Wulker. Looks like an underfed accountant," Antony said. "There's another guy. Big guy. Doesn't say much. Clean-shaven blond guy that came around with a woman around a couple of times. A tall blonde. Nice to look at."

"Have you seen anyone with weird throat tattoos?"

"Yeah sure. Most of them don't get seen again, though. What is it? Like a brand or a tag for a gang or something?"

"More like a brand," Ana said, drawing a deep breath. "It's dangerous."

"The tattoo? Do they contaminate the ink with some contagion or something?" Emilio demanded.

"Ehm. Well. Sort of?"

"But?"

"Here's where the woo-woo comes in."

"Ah shit. Don't tell us. If we get tattooed, we're screwed?"

"Yeah, pretty much."

Clanging signaled the guards' return.

The doors squealed open, blinding everyone again as the bowls were collected.

A new figure appeared in the illuminated rectangle of the doorway.

"Shit, Ana, that's him. The Accountant."

Ana's breath caught as she squinted to make out details as her eyes tried to adjust to the light. The silhouette was smaller than the guards, his form outlined in a suit.

"That one," his accented, nasal voice commanded with a nod.

The two guards collecting the bowls moved toward Ana.

"Oh shit, no, Ana!" Antony yelled, swiping ineffectually at the guards to stop them.

"Hey!" Emilio and the crewmen shot to their feet. "Leave her alone."

One of the armed guards dropped the point of his rifle at Emilio. "Back off."

"Emilio. My team is coming. Be ready for them. They'll need all the help they can get from the inside when they get here," she whispered, raising her hands submissively as the guard grabbed her wrist. "Woo-woo or not, be ready."

The guard wrenched her wrist painfully, dragging her out of the box into the garish fluorescent lights of a massive warehouse.

Ana squeezed her eyes shut against the pain from the light stabbing her eyeballs, alternately squinting until they adjusted.

The nasal voiced man questioned another larger figure standing further away, who appeared to just nod.

"Analiese Ortega."

"Yes?" she blinked at the man who wasn't much taller than herself. "You are?"

Creepy Accountant seems about right.

"Here to collect my leverage." He grinned and turned on his heel.

Shoved by a guard, she had no choice but to follow him as the steel doors clanged shut again.

"Don't worry, Ana, I'm right here with you," Antony said as they passed the taller man that fit the description of the second man Emilio described. "I'm not going anywhere."

The man's eyes slid from Ana to Antony.

"Does he see me?"

The corner of the blond man's lips lifted.

"Shit," Antony said.

Ice slid through Ana's veins.

The armed guard shoved her forward again, forcing her to keep up with the Accountant.

JOEY KANE PACED BEHIND her desk as her team assembled in her office. Jack Maeda was on the line from his New York office.

"Please close the door," she said to Aaron Connor as soon as he jogged into the room.

With a nod, he did so and moved in.

Joey's gaze slid from team member to team member. Even the ones that usually masked their emotions exuded concern. Aaron Connor, Raya Burns, Carson Perenga, Lirikai of the Barra'kidai, Ian McLachlan. Everyone else associated with the case was still in the field.

Do I tell them about the Gate?

She bit her lip.

No, there will be time for that later. Focus on this *case right now.*

"We're all here, boss," Aaron prompted, fingers tapping against his thigh.

Right.

"Jack is on the line with us," she gestured toward the conference speaker phone on her desk.

"Ana and Magnus?" Carson leaned in.

They were all clearly impatient for a status report.

"Dark."

The team erupted, all speaking at once.

"Fuck," Raya said.

Carson said, "When are we going in after them?"

"They should have been back by now," Aaron picked up Joey's pacing across the back of the room.

"Yes," Joey nodded. "They should have. The seaplane they used to fly into Barentia hasn't been returned yet."

"What do we know?" Jack's voice came through the speakerphone.

Joey hardened her voice. "First, we know they are both highly trained agents and that if they're in trouble, we need to give them time to resolve the situation. So we prepare in the event we will have to go in—and it looks like we may," she added before anyone could interject. "But we have to be careful."

"Fucking politics," Ian growled.

"Yes. Fucking politics," Joey repeated and reminded them of what they already knew. "While we have access to most waters, there are still some jurisdictions we are not free to enter without permission or a very good cause."

"And you know we can get in undetected," Carson said. "So, where is the problem?"

"Do any of you know much about the Barentians?"

Aaron and Raya were the only ones that nodded.

To the others, Joey briefly explained their history and relationship to outsiders.

"So grumpy, xenophobic polar bear shifters," Lirikai said.

"But why? The other polar bear communities don't go to the same extremes to keep outsiders away," Raya asked. "What are they hiding?"

"Everyone has their reasons to shut out the world," Ian said, casting Raya a grim look.

"What else do we know?" Aaron asked, bringing the meeting back to the point.

Jack filled in, "since Magnus identified Aksel Matochkin, our nearly dead shifter victim as his brother-in-law, we dug around into him. He and his sister Ulla are children of King Matochkin of the Novaya Zemlya polar bears. Their territory rides the line between the Kara Sea and the Barents Sea. Matochkin is notorious for his eccentricities and volatility."

"Seems an odd partnership for Thornsson to make," Aaron said.

"Magnus told me that his mother was from the Icelandic clan west of Barentia, while Ulla is from the southeast. Other ancestral matrons are from all over the arctic region, including northern Canada, Alaska and Russia," Joey said.

"Unions with each of the clans," Lirikai said. "Do you think Thornsson is planning something or expecting trouble?"

Joey hesitated, then blew out her breath. "Yes."

"Which is?"

How much do I tell them?

"Magnus' family has been the chosen guardians for an incredibly valuable artifact in the high north; only a handful of people in the world have some *hint* of its existence." She drew in a breath. "But our job is to focus on the human trafficking ring and rescue survivors in order to return them to their families. So, we'll focus on that."

Carson nodded, gaze locked on Joey's face. "You'll tell us about this artifact later?"

Joey resumed her pacing, ignoring the question. "Jack, what else do we know that can help us?"

"Matochkin is known to have worked closely with a company that provides renewable energy and satellite connectivity to remote areas like his. I sent you some files on that."

"Why is this of interest to us?" Joey reached for the device on her desk to switch on the monitor affixed to the wall, then the keyboard to retrieve the files Jack mentioned. On opening the file, several images cast to the screen, including the logo of an octopus with its arms enveloping a globe.

"Embraceable Energy. Embracing responsible technology to reach every part of the planet," Aaron said, reading the motto.

Jack continued, "I've had my tech team investigating to see if we could tap into this network. Most of the satellites in the north are government owned. Some allow us access, some don't. Barentia isn't covered because it's on a blackout list of protected areas."

"As per U.N. agreements with sovereign shifter nations. And?"

"And—."

"Look at the logo," Raya breathed.

Jack continued, "And the logo is suspiciously similar to the sigil tattoo."

Joey tapped a few keys to split the screen and bring up the images of the sigil. "Eight arms on the octopus. Eight bars on the sigil."

"Eight major shipping regions that we've seized human cargo from," Raya said.

"What do we know about the company's owner?" Carson asked, rubbing a hand over the back of his neck.

"Adolf Wulker. Shifter. Octopus," Jack said.

"Of course," Lirikai said, rolling her eyes.

Aaron resumed his pacing. "Why have we never heard of this guy before?"

"We're aware of him. We just didn't have cause to look into him before now," Joey said. "He's good at camouflaging himself and his activities."

"Slippery sucker," Lirikai said, crossing her arms.

Jack went on, "I've listened to all of Ana's interview recordings, including her trip into the astral realm with Aksel. She said the ocean was full of a black substance she wasn't sure was oil or ink. I think it was ink. Squid—Octopus ink."

"Meaning?" Carson glanced back to the enlarged image of the sigil.

"Meaning, I think Wulker is more than just a shifter. The sigils aren't just ownership brands."

"I'll have the medics analyze samples of Aksel's skin to see if they made the tattoo of squid ink and any other components," Joey said, following Jack's line of thought. "And if we can remove it."

"In the meantime, I'm going to have my tech department quietly poke around Wulker's infrastructure to see if they can find a way into his databases."

"Good," Joey said. "The rest of us are going to load the jet with gear and make our way to Norway. Whether Wulker has anything to do with the trafficking ring or not, we need to find out why Magnus and Analiese haven't contacted us via sat-phone. There could be a good reason they haven't reached out and I don't want to blow the mission if there is."

"And if not, we're ready to go in after them," Carson said, pulling Joey's attention.

He held her gaze.

She nodded, understanding that if she gave the order or not, he *would* go after Analiese.

"Dismissed." Everyone rose to clear out.

"I'll call in with an update as soon as we have something," Jack said.

"Prioritize this project above everything else."

"Understood." The line clicked off.

Joey turned, startled to see Carson waiting, hand on the doorknob. He closed the door, returning to speak to Joey eye to eye.

Carson's jaw tightened as he held her gaze, one fist enclosing the other as he considered his words.

Carson didn't look older than mid-thirties, like herself.

"We've both been on this earth for a long, long time."

Her lips quirked as she nodded toward the closed door. "Lirikai longer than you. I, a little longer than her."

His expression remained stern. "This artifact."

The two words stole away the budding smile.

"If this is what I think it is, Kane, it better not be the political road trap in our way of retrieving our agents. I don't care about that. Ana's life is worth more than that. And I'd have thought you'd feel the same about Magnus."

Joey's throat tightened. "I do. But, he also understands how important this is too, Carson. And yes, part of my hesitance *is* about the artifact. Magnus knows. He's always known. He will ride that line. That's why I'm giving him more time."

"If he lets Ana—."

"He won't," She cut him off. "He won't, Carson. I trust him as much as I trust you."

"If something happens to her…"

"I know. As I said at the top of this meeting, they're both trained agents. And I have to trust *them*. So do you. Now go and help Lirikai pack what you'll need. I can feel how close we are to shutting this case down."

Carson grunted, held her gaze a moment longer, then turned on his heel and left her office.

She watched him go, blowing out her pent breath, easing her hip against her desk. "Gods, please let this go the *right* way."

TWENTY

THERE WAS NO SENSE of time in the dungeon cell that they forced Magnus back into.

All he knew was that if he didn't find a way out, he'd die.

And that he stank.

When he wasn't plotting his escape, he was fantasizing about a hot shower with Ana. *His* Ana.

As soon as he ensured her safety. And he would, because he'd rip the world apart to find her. They *would* be reunited.

And when they were, he was going to take them both straight to the shower where they'd cleanse one another, and he'd worship her as he'd done the night before they flew out of Ireland for Barentia.

Only this time, he'd find all the little places he'd missed the first time.

Magnus never thought he'd find a mate. A true mate.

And a fragile human one, at that.

She fit so perfectly in his arms.

Their energies sparked similarly to how their bodies moved like they were made for each other.

Right from that first moment.

There was no way in all the frozen hells of the northern wastelands that he was going to find and then lose her.

First, he had to get out of here.

The metal tumblers in the lock clicked several times before dropping into place with a final clunk.

Magnus sighed and got to his feet, preparing for whatever came next.

The door didn't swing open like it had on previous occasions.

It drifted open, slow, tentative.

He grit his teeth, willing it to open faster.

What now?

A figure finally poked his head around the corner, expression uncertain.

"Elias?"

"Father." Elias pushed the door open the rest of the way, staring at Magnus, eyes flitting over the manacles and chains securing him to the wall.

The young man's eyes registered shock and sadness before quickly turning to fury.

"How dare they chain a member of the royal family?" his voice cracked as he surged forward.

"Which I no longer am, Elias," Magnus' own voice was calm and steady in the face of his son's outrage at his predicament. "Not as a banished one."

"Banished or not. You're still blood," he growled.

Magnus' heart soared with pride as he studied his son's face. His whiskers were starting. Patchy on the youth's smooth skin.

"Even if you are just here to spy on us."

Magnus' heart plummeted. "I came to sign the register."

"Why would you spy on us? For who? Mother says you can't be trusted."

"Since your mother is certain of these things, I'm sure she can answer your questions." Magnus glanced toward the door, half expecting her to come and send Elias away again.

"She isn't here. She left as soon as the guards confirmed you were chained and locked away."

Gone? Where would Ulla go? Why?

"And you've come down here. Why?" Magnus said, redirecting his thoughts to his son while he still had time to talk to him.

Elias shrugged. "I remember you. From before you left." He sighed, then cast Magnus a furtive glance. "I never could quite believe the things mother accused you of."

"I'm not surprised she spoke ill of me to you."

"She didn't. Not really. I, uhm, used to eavesdrop when she met with Grandfather. She would demand I stay in my room, but I never did."

"Like when you came to see me in the registrar's office."

Elias nodded.

"I see."

"She said you had spies sneaking around Barentia and that you would push Grandfather to give up the throne so you could have it. She said you were cold and calculating. That you were abusive during your marriage and would be again, should you be allowed to return."

"She said I was abusive?" Magnus gaped, then laughed.

"What's so funny?" Elias demanded. "There's nothing amusing about abusing your wife."

"No, Elias, there isn't. And I wasn't."

Elias glared at him imperiously. "Explain. I want the truth. I'm tired of everyone hiding everything from me. I'm not a child anymore."

Magnus considered this.

"No, you're not. And I saw that my fath—the king is very ill. You may ascend much sooner than I could have ever imagined."

"The truth. About mother."

"I never abused your mother. She would lose her temper and injure herself while striking me."

"You pushed her to it."

"No. I simply did not rise to her impulsive, unrealistic demands. I would not cooperate, and she would frustrate herself."

After a few moments considering this, Elias nodded.

He isn't blind. Thank the Gods.

Should I ask?

Magnus swallowed, chewing over the words.

"What happened to your grandfather? How long has he been ill?"

"I-I don't know. I don't know what's happening."

"Hasn't the shaman been able to do anything to help him?"

"The shaman is dead."

Magnus' heart skipped. "Dead? And no one has replaced him to ensure the king's strength?"

Elias shook his head. "Do you think Havard has something to do with it? Do you think he's betrayed us?"

"Why would you think so?" Magnus straightened his spine, mind racing.

The boy shrugged. "He's been... different. Different since Grandfather became ill."

"Do you know where your mother went?" Magnus said, bringing the conversation back to Ulla.

"No. Maybe."

"And she went with Havard and the other guards?"

"No, she went with Yvan."

"Yvan? Yvan Gorbinson, the stonemason?"

"No. Yvan Putinovski. Mother's human magician that she brought back from Grandfather Matochkin's court after you left—were banished."

"The king allowed a human magician in his stronghold?" Magnus gaped again.

"He's mother's trusted... friend. She was lonely, and he keeps her entertained with his tricks and illusions."

"Illusions?"

Awe slid across Elias' face. "Oh yes! He can create such wonderful images. Fill a room with beautiful colors, or make you believe you're in a place you're not. Even make himself seem invisible to the eyes."

"What else can this human magician do?"

"Oh, I have no idea, but he's very good at alleviating boredom. Or was, before mother had satellite television brought to the stronghold."

"What?" Magnus paced to the end of his chains, palms to face. "Forgive me, Elias. Did you say satellite television?"

"Yes, of course. Once the electricity was installed and proved to work, she arranged for other comforts."

Magnus glanced back at the light bulb. "What other *comforts* has your mother brought to Barentia?"

Elias smiled now. "We have internet from a satellite. The humans use snowmobiles to get around the island."

Humans plural? Snowmobiles?

"This doesn't make any sense. How long has all of this been going on?"

"Maybe a year or two? It took some time to have the work done to build the windmills and solar panels and run all the wiring through the stronghold."

"And your grandfather *allowed* all of this?"

"I *think* so?"

"This doesn't make any sense," Magnus said again as he resumed his short-strided pacing.

"He banished me for trying to encourage him to bring twenty-first century technology to Barentia."

"Mother has done a lot to negotiate with him *and* on his behalf. She arranged it all with this company that specialized in remote environmental access. They've done so much work, Grandfather gave them use of the smallest island at the northeast end of the archipelago."

"I see." But he didn't, really. Magnus' hands shook as he drew deep, steadying breaths. "Your mother arranged all of it?"

"Yes." Elias frowned. "She told him all about how this same company installed infrastructure all across Grandfather Matochkin's territory with brilliant success."

"And your grandfather didn't object to the idea of humans coming here?"

"Any outsiders that came into the stronghold were closely guarded by our men. Otherwise, they did most of the work outside."

"And they stay in Barentia?"

"Mostly at the base set up on the little island. But they periodically come onto the island proper, to train our people on how to do the maintenance."

Magnus snorted.

Un-fucking believable.

"What?"

Magnus just shook his head.

Bjorn Thornsson was so adamant that the island's borders remain closed—technological benefits or not — that he argued pretty damned hard with Magnus over it.

Having humans here—outsiders here — was what pushed him to banish Magnus. He was so paranoid about allowing anyone in. And now they were crawling with outsiders.

I guess he saw reason.

But not about me, apparently?

I'm still condemned to the mercy of execution.

Magnus dropped his head, shoulders bowed. The chains scraped on the stone floor.

He distrusts me so deeply, he would see me dead.

How did I fail him so badly?

He lifted his head, leveling his gaze at Elias.

Ulla has won. She has everything she could ever want or hope to have. She has my son. My father. The regency. The power to implement human comforts.

What's left?

Only direct rule.

Ice slid down his spine.

She wouldn't... would she?

No. She wouldn't. She at least had enough brains to understand that Barentians would rip her a part if she dared try to take it—even if something were to happen to Elias...

"What? Why are you staring at me like that?"

Magnus blinked.

He came here to find out how Aksel had ended up beaten to the edge of death, on a trafficker ship, with a tattooed sigil. And Havard, his father's personal guard.

Ulla had practically confessed to giving Ana over to them.

So this base that Elias mentioned had to be their center of operations. Hadn't it?

How far will she take this?

Does she want to rule Barentia herself, or destroy it?

"Father?"

"You shouldn't stay here."

"Mother doesn't know—."

"Barentia. You shouldn't stay in Barentia. You're not safe here."

Elias' gaze turned suspicious. "Are you insinuating that I can't trust Mother?"

Careful Magnus.

"You can't trust her friends."

"They're nothing. We're polar bears. They're powerless against us."

Sounds like something Ulla would say.

But Magnus had seen a lot in the decade since he left Barentia. Too much.

"They're not powerless, like you say. They did a lot of damage to your Uncle Aksel."

"Uncle Aksel? What do you mean? He's gone to visit Grandfather Matochkin for a few weeks."

"He's unconscious and under critical care."

"Wha—what do you mean?"

What do I tell him? Dear Gods, I never wanted to drag Elias into this madness.

He studied his son's face.

Not a child. Not anymore.

"Elias, I work for an organization that counter-acts human traffickers. I've been tracking them for years. These traffickers use a sigil to subdue and control some of their victims. When we found Aksel, he has a tattoo on his throat. Just like Havard."

"So, you *did* come here to spy on us," Elias' voice cracked as he paced back toward the door, hands curled into fists, checks flushed.

"Elias, these people—these friends of your mother's—have stolen a lot of people from their families. A *lot* of people. We've only rescued a fraction of those that were taken and sold around the world. These human *friends* are *not* powerless. They hurt Aksel. They've marked Havard, your grandfather's personal guard. What else have they done here?"

"Mother wouldn't let them—."

"She might not *let* them, but that doesn't mean they wouldn't try if she contradicted what they wanted. And those men set up on that little island you mentioned. I'm pretty damned sure that's what they're really doing. You're not safe here."

Elias stared at Magnus, chest rising and falling.

"You're just trying to trick me. Turn me against Mother and Grandfather."

"If my pack is still here and I think I saw Ana drop it before she ran, you'll find my satellite phone. Get yourself out into the clear, use it to call my team and they'll come and take you away to safety. Away from this group."

"You said they sell humans. So? What do I care?" Elias lifted his chin, eyes glittering.

"You don't mean that."

He shrugged, his face full of defiance.

"Leave me," Magnus said. "Just leave me alone."

"I have the right to be wherever I want and—."

"Get out," Magnus roared. He drew a breath, paused, then continued, voice so low it was barely a whisper. "Ulla gave my Ana to those traffickers. You refuse to listen to reason. I want to be alone in my last hours before I'm executed. Just leave."

Wide eyed, Elias backed out of Magnus' cell without another word.

Magnus doubted anyone had ever raised their voice to him, let alone roared in his face.

Right then, he was too heart-weary to care.

He slid down the wall and dropped his head in his palms.

He'd failed on all fronts of his mission. Lost everyone and everything—including his life.

TWENTY-ONE

"KEEP IT LOCKED," ELIAS Magnusson barked at the lockmaster, who accepted his order with a nod.

Elias jogged back up through the winding corridors of the dungeons, up the stone staircases and through the back halls to the family's private living quarters. Where his father should stay, rather than in a dank cell, chained with meteor metal.

He didn't stop until he was in the privacy of his bedroom, where he leaned back against the wall, chest heaving, both from the run and the shock of Magnus roaring full-bear in his face.

'Ulla gave my Ana to those traffickers.'

Would Mother do that?

Elias thought they just ignored the human world. It was of no consequence to Barentia. Except for entertainment. Yvan entertained his mother. Elias had satellite television to keep him entertained.

Entertained or distracted?

He'd noticed how easy it was to lose hours watching nonsense.

Nonsense that his grandfather would never allow.

Grandfather.

Elias felt the sudden urge to visit the old man. Guilt panged in his chest, realizing he had not visited him much since he fell ill.

He immediately left his room, striding toward his grandfather's. As he approached, Havard stepped away from the wall, blocking Elias' access.

"Havard? Step aside, I'm here to visit with my grandfather."

"He rests. You may come back later." He said, toneless.

"I won't disturb him. I just want to sit with him for a little while."

"Come back later when he's awake."

"But I—."

"No, your highness. He is not to be disturbed."

Elias blinked at Havard's denial of his order, refusing to move out of his path.

Havard had never refused him access to his grandfather before. Ever.

He stared at Elias as though he were just another servant. He didn't lower his gaze to meet Elias', as he used to do. Instead, he stood so that his body blocked the path, chin lifted.

Elias noted the black marking partially obscured by Havard's beard. "What new tattoo is that, Havard?" He gestured toward his own throat.

Havard glanced down at Elias then. Uncertainty glimmered in his eyes. "All of my sigils are representations of my lineages, or for my position."

"Huh, I've never seen that particular one. What is it for? It's new since the shaman left us. Who did the ceremony for it?"

Havard frowned. "It is a mark of my unfailing duty to my king. The regent had her trusted servant perform the ritual."

"I see." Elias said, swallowing. His shoulders twitched against the sudden tightening in his muscles.

Sacrilegious. A human outsider performing shamanic rites?

"Havard, has my grandfather mentioned when a new shaman will be chosen from our priests?"

The older man jerked his head in the negative.

"Are you sure I can't just slip in and sit with him? I promise not to disturb his rest."

"No." The scowl deepened.

If Havard won't let me in, I'll just go around him.

He turned on his heels, walking back the way he'd come, rounding the corner. He passed two other guards, neither of whom, as far as he could tell, bore the same tattoo that Havard had.

Another right turn and a quick glance up and down the corridor to ensure he was alone as he approached his destination. He tried the handle.

Locked.

No matter. Elias was deft with locks. Before his mother brought the outside world to his room with television, Elias had spent his life inside this stronghold. Locked doors meant something interesting.

He pulled his familiar long metal needles from his deep pocket, inserting them into the lock. With a few deft twists, the lock released, and the latch gave way under his hand. He dropped the lock picks back into his pocket as he pushed the door open, stepped inside and quickly closed it again before someone saw him, slipping the lock back into place.

Turning, he gasped.

The shaman's normally pristine quarters appeared as though a wild animal had rampaged throughout the space. His carefully cataloged library of books and scrolls was nearly empty except for the odd discarded, unrolled sheet lying haphazardly. The shelves of neatly labeled ingredients were even more bare. Furniture stood askew, pulled away from walls, drawers open, contents spilling out. Ancient tapestries torn from the walls, strewn around and discarded in heaps.

Tears stung his eyes as he stared.

He swallowed the revulsion of the disrespectful violation of the shaman's private rooms.

Who would do this? This domain should have been preserved for the use of the next shaman.

Elias sucked in a breath and approached the wall of solid oak shelves. He ran his fingers over the carved scroll work of leafy vines. Once he located the exact etched leaf he wanted, he pressed. It gave under the pressure of his fingertip, sinking into the polished wood until it resisted with only a click. One entire unit of shelves slid into the wall behind it far enough to allow a person to slip into the space between the front of the shelf and the back of the room's wall, still supporting the other shelves.

Elias' grandfather and the shaman had begun grooming him for kingship. That all stopped when the shaman suddenly died in an accidental fall down the servants' stairs. Then his grandfather had become ill and retreated into his private rooms, which Elias was about to enter from the secret passage that not only connected these rooms, but many others in the stronghold.

He was mindful to close the secret door before opening the next. That was the rule.

"Don't leave a gaping trail after you." His grandfather had said, when the two elderly men were divulging their secrets to him, once the serious training had begun.

Elias recalled how excited he'd been to stand in the narrow, darkened path, itching to explore anew. He'd thought he knew every nook and cranny of the stronghold. He'd been wrong. Happily so.

Does father know of these secret passages too?

He faced the second secret door in the blackness, surrounded by the sounds of his own breathing, which he willed to slow so that he could hear if anyone waited on the other side. He didn't want to run into anyone by accident.

Elias remained still, listening. Scenting. The tang of stone and ancient wood mingled with a millennium of dust tickled his nose and coated his tongue. There were only the lingering scents of his grandfather and the shaman's presence.

As far as he could tell, no one else had accessed this passage. He waited another moment in silence to ensure no one moved inside his grandfather's room before his fingers found the switch in the dark and pressed. He stepped away as the shelf-laden wall slid back as its opposite had done, and Elias slipped into the gap.

The pungent scent of illness was a thick cloud in his grandfather's room. There were no electric lights here, and only the fireplace cast some light from its neglected embers.

Elias pressed the switch to close the secret door.

He approached the bed on silent feet. His Grandfather's diminished figure slept under the layers of quilts.

Elias swallowed a gasp, blinking away the sudden onslaught of tears blurring his vision as he stared at the sallow face. He had looked unwell in the great hall. He looked even worse now.

His chest barely moved under the covers.

True to what he'd told Havard, Elias had no desire to disturb his grandfather's rest. He didn't bother moving a chair closer to the bedside. Instead, he knelt, resisting the urge to reach out to touch the elderly man.

Bjorn Thornsson was not a warm man by nature, but Elias had never doubted his grandfather's fondness for him. He'd felt it in the way he'd looked at him, the change in his voice when he instructed him, and the pride in his expression when Elias succeeded at a task. Occasionally, Bjorn would lay a hand on Elias' shoulder and often, that was enough.

He wanted nothing more than to feel that solid presence. That reassurance of his grandfather's strength.

Bjorn's eyes cracked open, and he tilted his head toward Elias.

"Elias," the older man said on an exhale.

"Grandfather," Elias whispered, trying to control the emotions choking him. "I didn't know you were so ill."

Bjorn's throat worked as though he struggled to work words up to his mouth.

Elias shot to his feet, rushing toward a small table bearing a pitcher and cup, where he poured water for Bjorn.

"Here," he eased his arm under Bjorn's shoulders to raise him enough to drink.

He took several tentative sips and closed his eyes with a sigh.

Elias helped him lie back, then returned the cup to the table.

"Grandfather, what has happened? The shaman is gone, you're ill, and Havard is behaving oddly. He's so determined to keep me out, I had to use the secret way in."

Anger flared in the old man's eyes as he reached toward his throat. His fingers shook as he pulled at the collar of his sleep shirt. "Can't..." he puffed, panting as he struggled to find words.

Elias gasped.

"... speak," he finally managed.

"The sigil. Is it magic?"

Bjorn gave a weak nod.

"What does it do? Havard said mother gave it to him for his dedication."

"Heh," Bjorn laughed, his head rolled from side to side. "No."

"But who? Why?" Elias asked, voice rising.

"Hshhh," Bjorn cautioned, hand wavering out toward Elias with his eyes closed.

He's so exhausted.

"Ulla."

Elias' entire body turned more frigid than any arctic swimming he'd ever engaged in.

No.

His mind raced.

It's not true. There's no proof. None.

Except for the strange tattoos that the shaman had not etched, by Barentian tradition.

No.

"Magnus?"

"Chained in the dungeon, waiting for his execution." Elias couldn't hide the bitterness from his voice.

Pain clouded Bjorn's eyes before he closed them. "Let him go. When your mother is distracted. Use the tunnels." He drew a deep breath. "Tell him... I'm sorry."

"I can bring him here to see you, Grandfather."

Bjorn shook his head. "No time. Let him go and...and you hide until he comes back for you."

Elias stared in confusion, heart pounding. "I don't understand."

"Promise," Bjorn panted. "I don't have long, Elias. Promise!"

"Sire?" Havard queried through the door. The latch turned, and Elias threw himself under Bjorn's bed. Havard's boots appeared, inches from Elias' nose. "Rest, sire. Mistress Ulla will return tomorrow with more medicine to give you strength to oversee the execution."

The edge of the covers shifted as Havard adjusted them over his king before returning to his post outside.

As soon as the door closed, Elias slid out from under the bed.

"Go," Bjorn said with some of his usual steel returning to his voice, though he kept it low.

"I can't leave you like this, Grandfather."

"I command it."

There was no more room for argument as Elias held Bjorn's clear gaze.

Deep down, Elias feared he wouldn't see his grandfather alive again. Shoving his dark thoughts aside, he said, "I love you, Grandfather."

Bjorn's expression softened as he brought his hand to Elias' cheek. "And I, you, my boy. Now save your father, since I can't."

TWENTY-TWO

ANA SAT ON A comfortable high-back chair, arms crossed, hoping she exuded enough boredom and annoyance to mask her anxiety.

Her captors had marched her through their operations complex in a warehouse and out to a pier, where they pushed her into a boat for a brief ride across a narrow stretch of water. From there, they led her to a small cottage overlooking the Barents Sea.

On reaching the small house, Ana turned back to see how extensive the island base camp was. Two cargo ships waited, with goods being shuffled across the compact harbor between them. She noted the logo on several of the shipping containers.

Embraceable Energy? Where Have I seen that before?

"I've seen it too," Antony said.

There was no time to ruminate on the familiar image as they shoved her inside the cottage and into her current chair.

They were all speaking English, and she guessed it was to intimidate her.

Hence her determination to look bored and annoyed.

Never let a predator smell your fear.

"I don't care if you think she has abilities. I want you to get rid of her," Magnus' ex-wife, Ulla Matochkin, said, scowling in

Ana's direction. "She has no use to any of us other than what you can get for her on the black market. *Sell* her."

"Ulla," the creepy accountant, Adolf Wulker's, voice was placating as he looked her way. "We can use her as leverage first."

"And I told you, whatever you think Magnus knows about this old thing Yvan is looking for doesn't matter. He's a stubborn bastard that won't tell you anything. I know him. He'll go to his execution in silence just to spite me."

Execution? Ana's hands fisted before she forced herself to unclench them.

"Oh, that doesn't sound good," Antony said. "Sounds like your rescue party hit a snag."

He's not my *rescue party. I'm* his.

Antony snorted. "You're going to rescue the big polar bear shifter from an island full of more polar bear shifters and whisk him away to safety? Right."

The big guy strolled into view from somewhere behind her chair, grinning down at her.

Fuck, I forgot about him.

"Me too, sorry Ana," Antony said, looking contrite.

He laughed, drawing Matochkin and Wulker's attention. "What's so funny, Yvan?"

"She thinks she's going to escape and rescue Bjornson," he said, in heavily accented English.

"Ridiculous, why would you say that?" Matochkin said, her expression incredulous.

"Her ghost friend said so."

The tall blond woman approached Ana, eyes narrowed. "Magnus said that you—." She glanced over her shoulder at her partners before turning her full attention to Ana. Her eyes glittered dangerously; color infused her cheeks as she dropped her voice. "Magnus said you can astral travel."

Ana hesitated, but nodded.

Matochkin straightened. "Leave us," she barked at the men.

They moved closer to the women, brows raised at Ulla's tone.

The three of them towered over Ana's chair.

"Ulla, darling. She's my property to do with as I please. You said you had no use for her when you gave her to me. Why the sudden change of mind?" the creepy accountant said, sliding a hand across Ulla's shoulders.

Ana almost leapt out of her chair at the sight of his hands shifting—separating into tentacles, massaging the woman's narrow shoulders and neck with intimate familiarity.

Oh gross!

She struggled to control her gagging revulsion.

"Ugh!" Antony echoed the sentiment.

"Besides, we have no secrets between us, right, my love?" Yvan said, caressing her face and kissing her mouth. "Whatever she has to say, we can know, too."

Ulla immediately relaxed her body. "Just five minutes. Female to female."

The men exchanged looks, released her, and moved toward the door.

Yvan stopped next to her chair, crouched so he could look her in the eyes and as he placed his large hand on her knee, he said, "If you say anything that upsets our Ulla, I will extinguish your ghost friend into oblivion and snap your neck so you may join him. I don't care how much money Adolf thinks he can get for you. I will do this." He gave her knee a single pat, rose, and left. The door closed with a soft click.

Ulla said, "You don't need to worry about Yvan. If you don't answer my questions, *I'll* snap your neck myself."

"Charming bunch," Antony snorted.

Quip all you want, it isn't your neck on the line, now is it?

"Nope, just oblivion, apparently."

"What do you want to know?" Ana said to Ulla, wondering if she could use this new situation to her benefit.

Ulla glanced at the door behind Ana. "Magnus said you spoke to Aksel in the astral realm."

Open desperation replaced the bitter scorn in Ulla's face. Her gaze flicked between Ana and the door.

Ana nodded.

"He's alive," Ulla said with guarded relief.

"He was then. That was days ago."

"And he had a mark on his throat? And don't lie to me or I'll—."

"Snap my neck, I know. And yes, he did. It prevented him from shifting, so he couldn't heal."

Ulla reached for the chair adjacent to Ana, sagging onto it. All the color drained from her face. "So it's true. He wasn't lying." She jumped to her feet, hands shaking as she paced the room.

"How can we remove it?" Ana forced as much calm into her question as she could.

"I don't know," Ulla said, her hand pressed to her forehead as she glanced at the door again. "I don't think it can be, not without a shaman, anyway." She drew a long breath, straightening her spine as her gaze searched the room, as though the answers were somewhere within it.

"Even if you decide to snap my neck, at least let Magnus go. Let him find a shaman that can help your brother. You *know* he would. Won't the king's shaman help him?"

"He's dead," Ulla said, resuming her pacing with a heavy sigh. "You know what? It's too late. It's too late for Aksel. I can't do anything to reverse it. I can't help him. It's too late."

"What's too late?" Adolf asked as he and Yvan entered the room.

"It's too late for her to *try* to bargain with me," Ulla said quickly, masking her emotions as she looked at Ana.

"Ah, well, did she tell you what you wanted to know at least?" Yvan asked, lacing his large fingers together as he moved into Ana's line of sight.

"No," she said, shrugging a shoulder. "I'm bored. We should find out what Magnus knows about this old artifact you want, so Adolf can sell her, and I can think about other things," she said to Yvan.

"Like becoming Queen." Yvan grinned, trailing a finger over her cheek.

She twitched away from his touch, seemed to catch herself, smiled, and placed a kiss on his finger. "Exactly."

"I like this idea," Yvan said, leaning in to nuzzle Ulla's neck.

Ana looked away, in a bid to control the returned revulsion churning in her gut.

I don't think I can take any more of this.

She glanced up to see Antony looking as ghostly green as she felt.

You should check on Emilio and the guys in case they decide to move them. If I survive this, I'll need to know where to direct my team.

Antony's hesitation was clear as he looked between her and the three lovers, pretending to have forgotten about her.

I'll be fine. And even if I'm not, you can't do anything about it, Antony. Don't get obliviated—if this guy isn't talking out of his ass.

Antony snort-laughed, then snapped his mouth shut when Yvan turned his attention on him. "Okay, stay alive," he said and blinked out of sight.

"Where's he gone, your ghost friend?" Yvan demanded.

"With the three of you heating things up in here, he didn't think he wanted to stick around if squid boy over there broke out the rest of his tentacles. So, he abandoned me to suffer alone."

Yvan backhanded Ana, snapping her head to the side with a crack. Her head rang as pain bloomed through it from the impact on her cheek.

"Don't damage my property!" Adolf shot forward, grabbing her face and looking at either side. "You're lucky you didn't break her. Now I'll have to wait till the bruising clears up before I can present her to the special clients I contacted. Damn your temper, Yvan. They don't like it when I tease them and delay presentations longer than necessary."

"I don't care about your vast network of clients. I promised the others we'd find the artifact and secure it. This is all I want, Adolf. Not money, like you."

"It's not just the money, Yvan." Adolf stepped closer to Yvan, snarling up at the taller man's face.

Ulla slid between the two, her bottom against Yvan's groin, her breasts to Adolf's chest, distracting both.

"We all want something, don't we? How about we head back to the stronghold and see if we can finish what we started? Yvan's right, we should bring the human woman, although I doubt the leverage idea will work. I have something else in mind for her." Ulla glanced Ana's way, leveling her glittering blue eyes at her.

Uh oh.

I DON'T CARE WHO comes in here next. I'll rip their head off if I have to, in order to escape and find Ana.

Thoughts of Ana being trapped on a ship like the ones they had seized over the last decade made the bile in his gut rise.

I have to get out of here.

But no matter what he tried, despite knowing better, he could not slip out of the manacles, nor break them. All he'd earned for his trouble were very sore wrists and ankles and a chipped tooth, with barely a scuff on the meteor metal.

He'd cursed his ancestors repeatedly for their exquisite skill in metal craft and shackle design and quality.

These are probably the original damned shackles from when the cell was built.

When he wasn't plotting his impossible escape, he calmed himself with fantasies of Ana and her sapphire blue panties, which turned out to be counter-productive and incited the urgency to escape all over again.

But then, there wasn't anything else to do. The chains were almost too short for push-ups.

Suddenly, the lock tumbled with a snap, and the door banged back against the stone.

Magnus was on his feet, ready to detach heads.

Elias stood, wide-eyed and panting. To the lockmaster he said, "tell them I stole the keys and knocked you out or something."

"But your highness—," the lockmaster protested.

Magnus eased back on the readiness to do violence. "Or go into hiding until this all blows over. You know they'll torture you for information if they catch you."

"Shouldn't I rally the guards to protect you?"

"They will follow their commander and they don't understand that he is compromised," Elias said, stepping into the cell. "I don't want the stronghold in an uproar when I'm trying to help my father escape quietly. Which key is it?"

The lockmaster freed Magnus in seconds.

"He's right. Hide yourself and your family. Once I get out, I will be back—and not alone."

"Yes sir. But I still think we should rally support. Not all Barentians agreed with the banishment and certainly many are not pleased about the scheduled execution."

"Nor am I, but please, take your family and go."

The lockmaster dropped his precious keys into Magnus' hand and disappeared.

His fist clenched around the ring of keys. Centuries old. He laughed.

Elias gave him a quizzical look from the door, his impatience to be away evident.

"Of all the plans I had to escape, not one of them included having the keys dropped in my hands and just being set free."

"Grandfather told me to take you through the tunnels to escape."

The tunnels! Dear Gods, I've forgotten about the damned tunnels!

"He did?" Magnus stood rooted in place.

Elias nodded, glancing up and down the corridor. "Yes, he ordered I set you free. So let's go, Father."

Magnus couldn't believe what he was hearing.

A second later, Elias' hand grabbed his wrist and yanked him toward the door.

Magnus had enough brain function to close and lock it before following his son down the stone corridor toward the hidden entrance of the tunnels. Neither spoke as they made their way, careful to avoid passing guards who were fulfilling their duties.

Only the royal Barentian family were aware of the secret tunnels beneath the stronghold that led through the mountain and out to a tiny inlet on the western side of the island. The path hadn't been needed in centuries because it had been that long since the stronghold had failed to keep invaders out.

Down the next corridor, the scent of alcohol signaled they were close to the tunnel entrance. Stacks of barrels crowded the narrow space. With a quick glance up and down the hall, Magnus shifted his hands, extracting his bear claws and drove them into the backs of some barrels, causing them to leak so that the pungent aroma would mask their personal scents.

Magnus led the way into the very back of the barrel cellar, squeezing between the largest ones with the thickest layers of dust. "Dwarven Ale," he murmured as he shimmied around behind it and along the wall to the dark corner. With no light source, he had to feel around for the correct stones. Magnus funneled his bear magic into his paw, extending the powerful claws in order to pry the stones loose, as he used to do in his youth.

He ignored the pang of nostalgia and focused on the genuine sense of urgency to move unseen and unheard.

"Got it," he grunted as the stone finally gave way, and then the next. With limited space, he only removed as many as was necessary for Elias and himself to crawl through, then pulled them back into place, using the meteor metal handles affixed to the backs of the stones for that purpose.

"Your pack is just up along here," Elias said, taking the lead through the tunnel. "I brought it down from the internal passages before going around to fetch the lockmaster."

"Thank you, Elias." Magnus blew out a breath, unable to see much in the dark. Both used their heightened sense of smell and hearing to navigate, guided by the changes in air drafts and echoes from the rooms above.

By the time they reached the pack, their eyes had adjusted enough to register slight variations in the dark.

Elias said, "After we last spoke, I went to see Grandfather. He's not well. I don't think he has long. He commanded I set you free, and to tell you he was sorry."

Emotions punched Magnus in both gut and chest, making it difficult to breathe. His father had never in his life apologized to anyone.

"He's dying?"

"Yes." Elias' voice sounded small in the confined space, reminding Magnus how young he was, despite his growing body. "And he's marked, like Havard. It was hard for him to speak. I wanted to take you to him, but he insisted you escape. He said you'd come back for me and that I was to hide until you did."

Magnus' heart pounded in his chest, torn between escaping to find Ana, getting Elias to safety, and seeing his father one last time.

One thing he never dreamed of was his father's death. He'd always thought of his father as eternal.

Foolish. Childish.

"Does your mother know about the tunnels?"

"No. Grandfather and the shaman expressly forbade me from sharing their existence with her or anyone else."

"Good."

"Can we take him with us, Father?"

Get Elias to safety and call Kane, or go back for his father? The sooner Kane and the team arrived, the much better chance they had of tracking Ana.

"Have you ever made the swim to Bear Island? It's a hard journey. Long."

"Twice. Grandfather said it was a tradition that every young bear makes the swim. I almost failed the first time, the second was much better. I made it there and back the same day."

Pride threatened to burst Magnus' chest at his son's words.

A strong swimmer. Good.

"Listen carefully, Elias, this is very important, and I want you to do exactly as I ask. Will you do that?"

"What do you want me to do?"

Magnus noted he didn't agree, but went on anyway. "I want you to run to the exit point. There should be a small boat stored in a safe place. Only after you ensure you are alone, row out to sea until you are clear of the island and use the satellite phone to contact my team."

"Okay."

"Identify yourself. Tell them Ana might be detained on a small island in the northeast sector of the archipelago."

"What about you?"

"Don't worry about me. As soon as you make the call, row the boat toward Bear Island, conserving your strength for as long as possible. Make sure no one sees you. This is vital, Elias. They *will* go after you."

"But I can help —."

"It doesn't matter that we're mighty polar bear shifters if there are so many humans, as you say. They will be armed with weapons that can kill us. I don't want any Barentians killed if I can do this discretely. Understand?"

"I understand," he said, but Magnus knew he didn't like it.

"When you're ready, shift into your bear and swim the rest of the way to Bear Island and wait. Just be a bear for a while. A few days if necessary. The local fisherman and environmental research crew won't bother you."

"That sounds lame. When do I come back?"

"You don't. You wait for me or one of my team members to come for you. The GPSA will keep you safe. No matter what, do not come back."

Magnus stared into his son's face, recognizing his own prideful stubbornness in his eyes. "Promise me."

Elias remained silent for an eternity before he finally answered. "Please save Grandfather if you can."

"I will try."

Elias suddenly gripped Magnus in a bear-hug, squeezing the air from his lungs. "Be safe, Father."

"Be safe, Son," he said, hugging his boy as tight as his boy hugged him.

Elias released him just as suddenly, grabbed Magnus' pack and ran down the tunnel. The run to the inlet would take many hours through the darkness.

Magnus had to trust his son would be safe. He listened until Elias' footfalls faded, then made his way along the tunnel back toward the junction that would give him access to the heart of the stronghold.

And to his father.

TWENTY-THREE

ANA HATED SNOW. AND she hated snowmobiles.

The one they'd forced her onto whined loudly and set her teeth on edge. Even more so now that it was no longer a source of potential escape, but one of further imprisonment.

She hated snow and cold. She hated the north and longed for her beachside home. The warm California sun, not this watery *sort of* light of the high north. Some people thought the high north was beautiful.

Beautiful?

Way up here in the wastelands of snow and ice and rock and nothing else?

They hit another bump, jarring her teeth as her helmeted head hit the guy's back in front of her.

She still wore the clothes she'd arrived in, the boots and jacket. At least she had that to fend off the cold, but didn't seem to be enough.

I've been cold since we disembarked from that damned seaplane. Where the hell is it, anyway? Had someone stolen it? Or maybe they just let it drift off to sea.

She almost laughed to herself, picturing some arctic wildlife riding the drifting craft around from sea mass to sea mass until it bumped up against an iceberg somewhere.

She thought of Aksel.

Her amusement died.

Would they do the same to her?

I couldn't bear to be locked inside my head like that. Especially not in a cold sea of icebergs.

Her worst nightmare, after the night terrors of Antony's accident.

Those had been horrendous. But at least now she understood he'd been trying to reach her. Show her what had happened.

But in the end, here she was. On a damned snowmobile, heading for what? Some sort of negotiation to force Magnus to tell them about some old antique thing before they killed them both?

No, they wouldn't kill them if they didn't have to. They'd subdue them and sell them to the highest bidder.

Like Emilio and the rest of Antony's crew would be sold off, eventually.

Unless Ana could get word to Carson and Kane and the others that it was all here. All this time. And they could end it all.

There hadn't been enough time, and she hadn't had enough energy to do an intentional reading of the place, but she was certain all the stolen victims had passed through this little island on their way to their buyers.

They hit another bump followed by a drop and Ana thanked God she didn't bite her tongue again or lose that little bit of gruel she'd had for breakfast.

That would be so gross inside this helmet.

Another sharp turn, another drop.

I'm gonna throat punch this guy as soon as he stops this goddammned thing.

The others rode identical vehicles behind her, fanned out so that if she'd tried to jump off, they'd either run her over or scoop her back up. And she didn't want to give Yvan the satisfaction of tying her to the damned thing.

They rounded another snowy bank of nearly black evergreens, and the stronghold came into view.

It was still impressive the second time, but now her foreboding intensified.

This time, the bad guys had her, and they were going to use her to force Magnus to give them information. They also had control over an entire clan of polar bear shifters that no longer owed allegiance to Magnus as a banished one, let alone one who, it seemed, was now on death row.

We're so screwed.

"Screwed, but not alone," Antony said, floating at warp speed beside her.

She almost jumped out of her skin, jerking the coat of the asshole driving the snowmobile so hard that he almost lost control.

He snarled at her with a few rude words.

You shouldn't be here! That Yvan guy said he can send you to oblivion. Go back and keep an eye on your crew.

"You don't believe that, do you? I think he's full of shit."

I don't know and don't want to risk it. Stay away from him!

Antony glanced back at the snowmobiles following behind. Concern crept into his expression despite his bluster.

"I'm going to check out this castle they're taking you to. Maybe I'll find you a way out."

He blinked out of sight, and Ana's snowmobile hit another bump.

ADOLF WULKER REMOVED THE helmet and dropped it on the seat of the snowmobile.

This is such a waste of time.

He was still fuming that Yvan had dared damage his property. Now he'd have to wait before presenting the little psychic to his favorite buyer.

A special buyer that would pay top dollar for her kind of novelty.

So now that he had to wait, he might as well indulge Ulla and Yvan in this little side project.

He signaled to Yvan that he wanted a few words once they went inside.

Adolf was worried about the subtle changes in Ulla since her brother had not contacted her. Her response to their touch, their usual means of keeping her happy, had cooled.

Does she know something?

Was she asking the psychic to use her ability to learn more about Aksel?

He threw his gloves down with a sigh.

She's going to be furious about what we've done to her brother.

Absolutely furious.

She would find out eventually. They just needed to keep her ignorant long enough for her to serve her purpose in their plans for *The Consortium* and, by extension, for themselves.

He followed the others inside the stronghold, ignoring the Barentian guards. So long as they were with Ulla, their regent, he and Yvan wouldn't be bothered by the dangerous shifters.

He tamped down his nerves under their disapproving glares.

The partners still needed her for a little while longer.

They'd already scavenged the shaman's grimoire collection, which had boosted his own ability beautifully and afforded them some level of safety, with both the king and the head guard under their control.

Still, Yvan was insistent they keep Ulla placated until he found the location of the artifact he was looking for.

Yvan fell in stride alongside Adolf. They slowed their pace until the others were out of earshot and no one else was close enough to overhear.

Adolf kept his voice low. "This device you're looking for. You're sure it's here?"

Yvan nodded, studying Adolf's face. "What are you worried about? We're very close, I can feel it."

It was some kind of access device or gate or key to another world. Adolf didn't know the details, he was too busy running his business.

He knew just enough to confirm that he wanted to be part of it. A prime opportunity for expansion. So he kept Ulla happy, Yvan happy, and *The Consortium* happy. Wins all around.

They continued walking toward the king's reception room next to the larger great hall, before ordering Ulla's ex-husband to be brought to them for questioning.

They wouldn't all fit in the dungeon cell.

"I'm concerned about the strength of my networks and my control over them as my venom thins," he spoke to Yvan, voice low so it wouldn't carry along the stone corridor to the shifters' sensitive ears.

Bringing energy solutions to the worlds' remotest areas had given him all the access he needed to thrive, both legitimately and illegitimately.

His network truly was global.

"With access to wherever this artifact connects to, you can expand. The opportunities are endless," Yvan reassured him.

Adolf loved the idea of endless opportunities.

"What kinds of merchandise will we find on the other side of this thing, do you think?" He imagined a whole new world of beings he could add to his catalog. "Yes, more novelty. More... unique acquisitions would do nicely."

"We've listened to Conrad brag endlessly about this powerful being he's controlled for centuries. Look at the power he has."

Conrad, a member of *The Consortium*, had manipulated a Djinn—if Adolf recalled correctly—into bestowing powers and longevity on him before he entrapped and siphoned her power for himself.

That's what Yvan wanted. He wanted to control powerful creatures like that for himself, boosting his own power.

"And you believe there are more like his creature, accessible through this gate?"

Adolf enjoyed a different kind of power. Power over the fates of the lesser and the powerful alike. Merchandise and buyers, there was little difference to Adolf.

A shiver rippled through him.

He provided services that fed his own sense of power.

They entered the room. Adolf watched the psychic as they settled in to wait for Ulla's ex-husband to arrive and tell them what they all wanted to know.

His gaze slid from the woman, returning to Ulla.

Her brother had been the last instance where he'd had to use his deeper ability to subdue a difficult situation.

He whispered to Yvan next to him, "The venom in my octopus ink is thinning."

"So you said before."

"My ability to overcome another's will is weakening. I've had to release some of my older connections in order to accommodate this last spell," he said, referring to Ulla's brother. "And the two before that. Shifter will is so much harder to control than human will."

Yvan scowled as his eyes flicked between Ulla and Adolf.

Neither Adolf nor Yvan were sure what had set off the polar bear shifter, but he'd gone on a rampage in the facility, screaming about one of Adolf's products. They subdued and spelled him, then put him on a ship. A ship which was eventually seized, and no one had heard from him since.

"Each time I used my venom to calm another, it drew on my strength, even with the spells you used to boost it. I'm stretched too far. My connections are thinning to fragile filaments; any more, and they may snap. I have no way of knowing what will happen. Could be some, could be all."

"Or drain you to a husk. I've seen it with other magic users that weren't strong enough to maintain their spells."

Adolf wasn't sure he liked the calculated look in Yvan's eye. "We're almost finished here. Once I have control of the artifact—on behalf of *The Consortium*, of course—it won't matter."

"If we can't control the king and his guard, we can't control the rest of the Barentians. If we can't control the Barentians, we sure as hell can't control the rest of the polar bear clans, who will no doubt want to overrun the territory for themselves. They won't stand by while humans take over."

"Once I have the power we're seeking, they'll do whatever we want them to."

"Are you so sure about that?" Adolph adjusted his posture on his seat, turning more fully toward Yvan as his agitation got the better of him. "Didn't one of *The Consortium* members say that we are ensuring control of the artifact for when it awakens? Meaning we won't have access to power right away?"

Yvan shrugged, scowling at Adolf's line of questioning. "Maybe. Maybe not. The shaman's books have histories and detailed spells to connect and use the thing. There just hasn't been enough time to read through them all yet. Ah, finally." He nodded toward the door.

Adolf turned his attention to the door as two guards appeared with grim expressions.

There was no chained Barentian polar bear shifter behind them.

"Where is he?" Ulla demanded, striding toward the guards.

"When we couldn't find the lockmaster to open the cell, we had to use the secondary key."

"And?"

"The cell is empty, mistress."

"Find the lockmaster," she roared as the guards rushed out, "Find Magnus!"

Adolf jumped to his feet when she charged toward Adolf's property, hand extended to grab her by the throat.

"Ulla!"

The woman, Ana, squeezed her eyes shut, stifling a whimper as she clutched the chair she sat on, head pressed into the back of it.

"Where is he?" Ulla demanded of the woman, shaking her.

"How the fuck should I know? I've been trapped with you assholes since you caught me at the fishing village," she forced the words out of her compressed windpipe.

Ulla shoved her as she released her, forcing the chair to rock backwards.

The woman clutched at her throat, gasping and coughing from the assault.

She'd have more bruises to add to her growing assortment.

More delays before Adolf could collect on her. His buyer liked his acquisitions pristine, unblemished.

"Will the two of you stop damaging my goods? *Please*," he shouted, no longer willing to conceal his exasperation. He sighed, running his fingers through his dark hair. "Control your tempers. Ulla, since your ex-husband appears to have escaped his inescapable prison and chains, where would he go? We're on an island. His choices are limited."

"He's banished. No one would dare defy the king's edict by helping him."

"Well, it appears the lockmaster has, or Magnus Bjornson overpowered him despite his predicament."

Ulla turned back toward Adolf's prisoner. "He knows his woman is bound for the black market. He'd go after her."

"So all we have to do is wave her around as bait to lure him to us," Yvan said.

Adolf said, "Ulla, you mentioned he had connections to the GPSA. If he brings them here, it would ruin everything I've—we've built. We're too close to lose it all now."

"Yes, so we have to find him as soon as possible," Yvan agreed.

Or I need to get out of here as soon as possible.

He glanced between his partners and his property seated across from him, weighing his options.

TWENTY-FOUR

"Jesus Christ, I had no idea the kind of shit Ana gets into in her line of work. No clue." Antony muttered as he drifted through the Barentian stronghold, seeking anything or anyone that could help him help Ana escape this crazy situation. "This isn't what normal people do."

All the time they'd lived together, when he was on shore leave, he'd always thought Ana was a ranked pencil-pusher at a government office in the town they lived in.

Boring, safe, easy.

"I thought *I* had the exciting life." He poked his head through a thick stone wall, expecting to find another bedroom. "Oh-ho! What's this?" he moved into the dark space between the rooms.

"Of course, an ancient castle has secret passages, on an island with people that turn into polar bears... and is aggressively occupied by a squid man that sells humans for money and a magician that can send me to oblivion. Of course." He threw his hands up in the air.

He followed the dark corridor to an intersection, where he saw movement. "I hope there aren't also giant-sized talking rats in this place. I don't think I could handle that." He drifted toward the movement, which turned out to be that of a large man.

Ana's large man.

Relief and jealousy ripped through Antony.

Relief because help was close by for Ana. Jealousy because her lover was close enough to rescue her while Antony couldn't.

Just because that guy had a body and Antony didn't. A very ripped body.

Yeah, he'd seen them in bed together. Accidentally. He wasn't a voyeur or anything. But it was enough to make him realize what he'd missed out on with the woman he'd never asked to marry him, and should have.

Instead, when she'd finally confided her secret ability to him, he freaked out like the coward he was and broke it off, convincing both of them that friendship was the best option.

Until she'd persistently tried to save his life with her warnings of the pending accident on his ship.

Such a coward.

"I never deserved her," he mumbled, following Magnus along the secret passages, hoping he was making his way to Ana to get her off this damned island so they could get back to the business of rescuing his men from the human traffickers.

His men. His crew were still alive because of her. And they would be rescued because of her, too.

"I know it. Just like I *know* you'll get her out of here," he said to Magnus' broad back, ignoring how much more muscle he had than Antony ever did.

Magnus paused, facing the wall, running his hands over the surface.

"You'd better be worthy of her, or I'll haunt the fuck out of you," Antony growled in his ear.

Magnus' head jerked toward the sound of Antony's voice. He stood still, listening, nose twitching as though he was scenting something.

"Did he hear me?" Antony waved a hand in Magnus' face.

Magnus turned back to the wall. After a moment, an audible click released the panel. He stepped aside as it backed into the space.

Antony passed through the wall ahead of Magnus.

An old man lay inert on a high bed, buried under several thick blankets which barely moved for the shallowness of his breathing. The room was dark except for the few embers amongst the ash in the great fireplace at the foot of the bed.

Someone gasped.

Antony spun as the panel eased back into place, showing a wall lined with heavy bookshelves. His gaze flicked around the room to determine the source of the gasp.

A second old man with a tattooed face and wild hair emerged from a corner, gaping at Magnus in shock and relief.

Magnus ignored this man, his focus intent on the bed, where he dropped to his knees with a low sob. Carefully, he eased the man's beard and sleep shirt aside, exposing his throat— marred by a black ink tattoo. Retracting his hand, the fabric and beard fell back into place, obscuring the mark.

"Father." He reached for the sleeping man's hand. He didn't respond when Magnus touched him. Magnus' breath shuddered as he leaned his forehead on his father's arm.

Antony looked away from the other man's pain, clearing his throat to ease the dense emotion from his chest. "Yeah, I've been there buddy. It sucks."

"Who are you?" The second old man was suddenly in front of Antony, forcing him back a few paces.

"Wha—You—." Antony waved at the old man's finger extended toward Antony's face. Their hands passed through one another. "You're dead too?"

The lively, dead old man puffed up with indignation. "How dare you intrude in this room! You are not Barentian. You're not even a polar bear. You're..." he looked Antony up and down. "Human."

"Yeah, so? It's not like I want to be here. I've got a friend in trouble downstairs and half a dozen more in trouble on a ship bound for the continent. And only *that* guy can help any of them." He jabbed a finger in Magnus' direction. "And yeah, they're *all* human, well, mostly human. And all want nothing more than to go home." At least he thought they were all human. Psychics were human too, weren't they?

"What do you mean, mostly human? Not a shifter? An elemental? A Fae? Sprite? Please tell me not a vampire. Or *another* one of those sneaky magicians."

"Wha—No, none of those." Antony's head spun. "The only magician I know of is that big Yvan guy who's holding my friend hostage. She's a psychic. I don't know if that's human or not?"

The old man nodded, grumbling. "Yes, human. Naturally enhanced but still human."

"Ah. Well, she can see me, so can you tell me how to direct her out of here if I can get her away from that bear woman, the squid guy, and the magician?"

The old man growled. "Those three are abominations to all of paranormal society. They stole my sacred work and twisted it!"

The gnarled finger appeared inches from Antony's nose again before it whipped toward the bed. "They violated our king! I will not rest until he is restored or avenged."

Antony approached the bed, peering down at Magnus' father, who reminded him far too much of his own. The urge to help was overpowering, but Antony already had folks that needed his help.

"How do we wake him up?" Antony looked up at the old man. "If we wake him up, he can stop them, right? He can stop them from hurting Ana or selling her? I need her to help me save a shipload of people bound for the black market."

"Hmm, filth," the old man muttered, "Filthy matter. But we don't get involved in human affairs. We have far more important things to protect."

Antony grit his teeth in frustration.

"What's wrong with the king? What did they do to him?" He tried again, hoping to find some angle that would benefit his mission to free Ana. "Maybe Ana can help?"

Antony didn't know how, but given they were in the king's room and this guy knew the place, there had to be some way.

"What about you? Are you the king's manservant? Is there some secret I can relay to Ana, who can tell Magnus?" He knew he was grasping. Desperate. But there just hadn't been anyone else to communicate with and he didn't know how much time Ana had left.

"Manservant!" the old man thundered, reminding Antony distinctly of all the dramatic movie wizards he'd seen in his life. "I am the king's shaman!"

"Shaman! You're a magic worker too, then?" He glanced at the King. "What happened? Why didn't you help him?"

The old man deflated. "I was already dead by the time they got to him and cast their twisted spell. I couldn't protect him like this. Not enough to keep him safe. My energy is keeping him alive as he is."

"Spell? Is it something we—you can teach to Ana to break it?"

"She isn't a Barentian priest."

Antony wanted to scream, but maintained his calm. "But the magician that cast this spell isn't either."

The tattooed old man tilted his head up, looking down his nose imperiously at Antony. "They stole our spells. I will only share our sacred knowledge with another Barentian."

"Even if it means saving your King? If we can get Ana in here and it works, you can help him."

"Or she would have the power to kill him and enslave the rest, starting with Magnus."

Antony stared at the highly paranoid old man at a loss.

Magnus got to his feet, rubbing the grief clear of his face, and straightened himself to his full height as he looked around the room, whispering to himself or to his father. Antony couldn't tell which.

First, Magnus moved toward the nearly extinguished fireplace, knelt and carefully lifted the substantial hearth stone, revealing a deep gap beneath.

Antony couldn't believe how easily he moved the stone without any noise or effort.

"Christ, I'd have dropped the damned thing on my foot and alerted the whole castle."

The old shaman grunted in response.

Setting the stone aside, Magnus reached in and extracted a black rock with a leather thong dangling from it. It resembled a shiny piece of coal. He looped it over his head, dropping the rock behind his shirt, then replaced the stone.

"What is that?" Antony looked to the old man for an answer, but received only silence.

Next, Magnus rounded the enormous bed, reaching behind the solid oak headboard, and extracted what looked like a wall stone.

"Now what?" Antony gaped.

Magnus removed a wrapped object, then replaced that stone, too.

At the foot of the King's bed, Magnus lay his hand over the sick man's covered foot. "If I cannot save you, I will ensure Elias receives these."

The king still did not stir.

"We should never have banished Magnus. Our greatest mistake. Greatest," the old shaman said, voice heavy with sorrow. "He would have made a fine King of Barentia."

Magnus triggered the secret door.

Antony spared the Shaman a last look before following Magnus into the passage. As soon as the panel slid back into place, Magnus revealed another hidden cavity where he slipped the wrapped object and concealed it.

That done, his stride more purposeful, he made his way along the secret passages with Antony at his back until they passed through an area where voices echoed along the castle's arteries.

Magnus found a small panel, slid it aside, and peered into the room below. Antony pushed his head through the wall.

They'd found Ana.

Despite her bruised face and throat, she looked angry. Very angry.

Magnus growled, low and loud. The sound traveled throughout all the corridors, secret and public alike, reaching every wing in the mountain-based castle.

Antony's incorporeal form vibrated with it.

The king's banished son was back, and he was pissed.

"All right. Let's go get our Ana," Antony said, fisting his hands.

MAGNUS SLID THE PANEL aside, peering down into the meeting room.

Relief flooded his chest on seeing she was here and safe, rather than on a ship bound for Gods knew where to be sold.

Ana sat, spine erect, shoulders set, glaring at the room's three other occupants.

She turned to address Ulla, which allowed Magnus to see her entire beautiful face.

Her bruised face and throat.

Rage ripped through him, expressing itself in a roar that shook the ancient stones beneath his splayed palms and fingers.

He fought the instinct to shift as he ran down the passage seeking the next exit point.

Reason quickly returned, overriding his animal brain, reminding him that he was in a castle full of Barentian guards that believed he should be in a prison cell awaiting his execution.

And he'd just alerted all of them with his very loud announcement.

Why is Ana here?

Ulla had told him that she was with the traffickers.

Having reached the next exit point, he paused to think.

She's being held captive. Here. With a bruised face.

Was there any other purpose than to draw him out?

To make a show of his execution? It would settle things for the succession after his father died, which might not be long.

Gods protect Elias.

His hand drifted over his heart as he made the plea, fingers grazing the stone beneath his shirt. The key. He'd hidden the book in the passage's darkness.

Instinct had bid him remove the sacred objects from his father's room for safekeeping. They couldn't be taken by anyone that couldn't be trusted with them.

Only a king and his shaman had the right to these artifacts.

He would ensure that Elias received them, or that no one would.

He removed the object from his shirt, and likewise hid it as he had the book.

The sounds of guards running and shouting orders met his ears as he waited.

As soon as they saw him, they would converge on him.

When they do, I just have to make sure I'm nowhere near a passage access point so that they won't discover the tunnels.

The secret tunnels led to the sacred gate for which he'd just hidden the key and spell book. The gate that his family had been charged with protecting for millennia.

I can't let that end here.

Kane was convinced *The Consortium* wanted access to it. She was in a race to discover all the gates around the world to ensure their safety before *The Consortium* found them. Before the portals awakened from their slumber.

I can't worry about that right now.

Ana was being held captive, and they still had a mission to complete. People to save—if he hadn't blown it already.

Could he convince the Barentian guards the king was spelled, as was their trusted chief officer?

I have to try.

As soon as the exterior corridor was silent, he eased his way out of the secret passage. Ensuring it was closed and invisible to the eye, he silently made his way down the hall toward the meeting room. In the distance, the guards continued their search.

TWENTY-FIVE

ELIAS' MUSCLES STRAINED AT the oars as he propelled the small craft along the rolling ocean surface. He'd already made the call to Magnus' contact. Kane.

He recalled that name. Kane was the woman that had spun his life in a new direction when she visited Barentia all those years ago.

It was her fault that he'd lost his father, and all of this was happening now. He was sure of it.

Despite his overwhelming bitterness when she'd identified herself on the satellite phone, he'd relayed Magnus' message, then continued his journey.

The bitterness fueled his muscles as he rowed because he had promised his father he would continue on to Bear Island.

His pride screamed to go back. To help. To save his grand-father and people from the humans with weapons that could kill them.

Surely they could overcome them with their great bear warriors.

No. He'd seen the movies and the news on the television. Their warriors wouldn't even get near the humans to tear them apart with their claws and teeth. How could anyone fight against that?

But Magnus is going to.

He glanced at the pack, wondering if there was a gun in it. He hadn't explored its contents beyond extracting the needed phone.

He kept rowing, returning his attention to the rolling line of the horizon and the misty bump that was Barentia.

Dots fanned the surface.

He squinted, but even his enhanced senses couldn't make out their shapes yet.

Birds? Dolphin fins, maybe.

The weak sunlight caught the shape of a sail.

Boats.

'They will go after you.' Magnus had warned him.

They would mark him like they'd marked his grandfather and Havard.

Elias swore as he reached for his boots and shoved them into the pack, then pulled off the rest of his clothes, adding them to his boots. Yanking the zipper closed, he spared the growing dots one last glance, unable to determine how many pursued him.

He held his breath, leaped into the frigid Barents Sea and shifted.

His hands extended and widened into powerful paws with deadly claws. The pads of his palms thickened and turned black, while translucent fur sprouted from every pore of his body.

Power and strength surged through his muscles.

Still buoyant, the pack floated on the surface as he drew a breath. Grabbing it with his teeth, he began the long swim to the safety of Bear Island.

Or so he hoped.

ANA'S BREATH CAUGHT AT the sound of the great roar reverberating through the stronghold.

Magnus!

She glanced up in time to see Antony leaping through the upper portion of the high stone wall, looking like he was ready to fight.

Ulla's expression registered panic as the sound continued.

Yvan's gaze focused on Antony's dramatic entrance.

Adolf slipped out of the door, with no one but Ana noticing his departure.

The sound of thunder echoed between the thick rock of the mountain's base and the stronghold's stones. Growing steadily.

"Choppers!" Antony whooped gleefully.

Yvan and Ulla exchanged confused glances.

"Where's Adolf?" Yvan demanded, moving around the table toward the door.

"I don't know. Grab the human. Magnus is coming for her," Ulla shouted.

"Yeah," Antony said. "And he's pissed."

"You saw him?" Ana gasped.

"I was with him when he found his father. The King is dying, Ana. I think he's going to rip these two apart when he finds them." His eyes glittered as he looked straight at Yvan. "Especially him."

"Why?" Ana asked, looking between Antony and Yvan, who stared back at him, color flushing his pale face.

"Who's she talking to?" Ulla demanded.

"The dead human who can't do anything to help her, or stop us."

"Oh yeah? I know the shaman you killed is keeping the king alive, and he'd kick your ass himself for violating their sacred culture."

"They killed the shaman?" Ana's voice rose with her shock.

"Yvan, I told you to grab her; take her to the hall where we can display her when we catch Magnus," Ulla commanded.

Yvan grasped Ana's wrist, wrenching her forward.

"Ana, you have to escape. Bring a priest to the king's chambers so they can reverse the spell that's killing him before it's too—."

Yvan shouted several words in a language Ana couldn't understand, swiping his hand through the air in Antony's direction.

"Antony!" Ana screamed as he sailed through the air backwards, disappearing through the wall.

Yvan yanked on her arm. She resisted enough to draw back her free hand, and when he yanked again, she used the momentum to launch her fist into his face, cracking his nose.

Pain lanced through her knuckles and up her wrist, but she didn't stop striking the much larger man, despite his rock-like face breaking her hand.

Grunting, he grabbed her other arm, and she went at him with her feet like the little hellcat that Magnus had accused her of being.

"Subdue her, now!" Ulla shouted.

Yvan barked a few words as his clammy palm clamped on her forehead.

Ana collapsed as the world went white.

ADOLF DROVE THE SNOWMOBILE hard, pushing its engine as fast as it would go, as he raced back toward his compound at the northern edge of Barentia.

"No, no, no!" He screamed as a heavy transport helicopter buzzed overhead.

GPSA.

He cranked the engine harder, determined to get to his ships.

There's only one helicopter. I have an army of men with plenty of guns that will take care of those agents.

By the time he arrived at the water's edge, the helicopter hovered over his warehouse roof as black-clad agents dropped to the building below while taking fire.

Good. His men were doing their jobs.

Roaring drew his attention to the open landscape beyond the small marina, where an aurora of polar bears churned up snow and rock as they sped toward his facilities.

Panic rising, he glanced back toward his island compound across the water.

One ship had already left the small port. The other was gearing up its engine. It would keep going despite the raid, as instructed.

Adolf ran the snowmobile as close to the dock where his small watercraft awaited him. Jumping on board, he engaged the engine and steered it toward the departing ship. As he sped toward it, he sighted a second helicopter in the distance and assumed it was searching for the first ship.

Eyes on the sky as he sped toward the closer ship, he didn't notice the massive roll of ocean water until it was too late.

Something large and gray barreled into his small boat, sending it flipping through the air.

Stunned, Adolf hit the water hard.

The shock of the cold water sent him to the surface, gasping for air. The large gray mass continued to circle him.

Not a shark or a whale.

He dropped below the waterline to see what blocked his path to escape.

He blinked. *What the fuck is that?*

He screamed ocean water as it turned and surged toward him, maw gaping, teeth extended.

He shifted instantly.

His slick body darted to the left, evading the jaws of the creature pursuing him. Extending one of his tentacles, he latched on to the back of the creature's neck with his suckers. Adolf ballooned the canopy of his body and enclosed his attacker's head so that it couldn't see. Wrapping the rest of his tentacles around its head and neck, he held on as it jerked left and right, trying to dislodge him.

Unable to, it swam toward the sound of the ship's motor, straight for the hull where a second creature similar in size but different in form appeared to push the ship's bow.

Fearing the creature would ram the ship head-first, which would crush Adolf, he let go.

The monster immediately twisted, though not before it impacted the ship, setting it to rocking.

By now, he understood these creatures were GPSA shifters intent on capturing his cargo.

Relieved that the ship didn't capsize, Adolf engaged his camouflage as he sank to the sea floor, creeping ever forward as fast as he dared, determined to catch the rudder and hide in a crevice. Even if they seized the ship, he could still escape.

A silver-scaled fish swam above him in the ship's wake. Adolf used it as cover until he made a dash for the gap between the rudder and the propeller and settled in the arch above the two, attaching every sucker, securing him to its surface.

The silver fish maintained its position, following the ship.

Suddenly, the propeller groaned to a stop. The ship continued to drift.

The distinct sounds of shouting and cheering echoed through the hull of the ship, amplified by the ocean surrounding it.

Adolf cursed that he'd lost another ship to the Global Paranormal Security Agency.

I can still escape.

A few moments later, a woman's voice traveled through the ocean water now that it was clear of the engine's vibrations.

"Okay Lirikai, track him, but don't eat him! Kane wants him alive."

Adolf did not know what that meant. He flattened himself against the rudder as much as his flexible body would allow.

The two larger creatures circled the ship in opposite rotations, capturing and rounding up Adolf's men as they jumped into the ocean to escape.

The silver-scaled fish drifted up to his level. From this angle, it was impossible to miss all of its razor-sharp teeth as it stared at him with hungry eyes.

His heart pounded as he considered his options, which were few. Very few.

A ghost-like figure drifted in next to the fish and grinned. "Gotcha. Go ahead, try to ink us, you little bastard, I dare you. She's hungry. *Really* hungry."

TWENTY-SIX

MAGNUS RAN INTO THE great hall, toward the door that opened to the meeting room, where Ana had been detained. A cluster of guards held fast, blocking the door with angled spears.

He stopped, spun around and moved further down the length of the great hall toward his father's throne.

As he'd expected, guards converged on his location and surrounded him in a semi-circle with the stone wall at his back.

I don't have time for this. They've already hurt Ana. Gods only know what else they'll do to her.

His mind slid away from thoughts of Ulla's partners marking Ana with a sigil too.

No, I won't allow that to happen.

But first, despite knowing his case was a lost cause, he had to reason with his kinsmen.

His father's castle guard spread out around him, every one of them grim-faced, fists tightening on spears, swords or other preferred dangerous weapons from ancient times.

"You don't have to do this." he said, loud and clear.

"Magnus, don't make this harder for us than it already is," Jan, Magnus' second cousin, said. "There is no joy in seeing you fallen so low, but our orders are clear. We must detain you by command of the king's edict, preceding your execution."

"Your king is under a spell and dying in his rooms at this moment." Magnus held his gaze, then looked into the eyes of the other men facing him.

"Ridiculous," someone to his right scoffed.

"Have you not noticed that your commander has a black sigil tattooed on his throat? That is not a Barentian rank symbol. It is a distorted emblem used to control him. My father—your King bears an identical one. As he fights its effects, it drains the life from him."

"Lies," another said, raising his weapon higher.

"You've all known me my entire life. Have you ever known me to lie?"

"Things have changed in the last decade, Magnus. As have you."

"I have," he conceded. "And you're right, things have changed a lot here. New humans roaming the island. Some sort of base set up on the farthest island of our archipelago, run by more humans, no doubt."

"The king allows it."

Magnus nodded. There was no denying that. "But why? And who among the Barentians have access to it? Any? I wager not."

"Mistress Ulla frequently visits the place."

"I'm sure she does." Magnus smirked.

"What are you saying, banished? Are you trying to sway us against your father and ex-wife? We understand your bitterness and jealousy in such a loss of pride. We understand your desire for revenge."

"That's not what this is," Magnus growled.

They were easing closer to him as they spoke, tightening the space.

Despite their weapons, he could take down about half of them in his polar bear form—if he acted fast.

Although determined to fulfill their duty, they didn't want to hurt him anymore than he wanted to injure them.

"Tell us then, Magnus. What is this? What do you hope to accomplish here?" Jan's voice was soft, leaning on their personal history as Magnus had hoped to do earlier.

Jaw clenched, he stepped back, heel striking stone.

The guards moved in closer. Their expressions didn't give away their nervousness, but he scented it.

He was bigger than they were and a fierce fighter. Men were going to get hurt if he resisted. They knew it. He knew it.

"I'm ensuring my son still has a Barentia to rule when my father is gone."

Some men registered surprise. They'd expected him to declare the throne for himself.

It was all he needed.

He shifted in a blink, swiped out with a great paw. Then the other, sending his kinsmen spinning in opposing directions before any reacted. Bracing a foot against the stone wall behind him, he launched himself forward, bowling some of the rest to the floor as he ran like a freight train over them, snapping bones as he went.

Several recovered from their shock, and abandoned their weapons to shift and give chase.

Magnus charged through the castle now. Alert guards, still in human form, moved along the narrow staircases and halls to intercept him on his way to his father's room.

As he ascended to a secondary landing, someone threw a spear. Its aim true, it embedded in his flank, causing him to stumble. He roared against the pain, dislodged it with a swipe and kept going. Blood flowed down through his fur, leaving splotching prints as he ran.

"Don't let him get anywhere near the king's chamber!" someone shouted.

Two bears blocked the hall. He knew them. He knew all of them. There wasn't a single bear on this island that he didn't.

He drew a deep breath, sprinted forward and lowered his head, aiming for the narrow space between them. The impact sent them crunching into the stone walls on either side. Pain wrenched Magnus' shoulder from the impact and the rending of flesh as one clawed at him to stop him. But they couldn't.

They wouldn't.

He knocked aside two more guards posted outside the antechamber to his father's quarters and slammed into the solid oak door. It gave way on the fourth hit, splintering inward, its pieces shattering against the interior walls. As the door gave, Ulla and Putinovski, with Ana draped across his arms, appeared from the opposite side of the antechamber, then ran into his father's room.

"Havard, defend your King with your life. Magnus is here to take the throne!" Ulla screamed before slamming the bedroom door closed.

The iron lock clicked into place as Magnus and Havard stared at one another. Magnus' sides heaved from the exertion of the run, the spear wound and damaged shoulder.

He already filled most of the small room. When Havard took his bear form, there wouldn't be enough space for two grappling bears.

Things were about to get messy.

And Ulla had just commanded him to fight to the death if necessary.

Given that she had just locked herself in his dying father's room with his vulnerable mate, Magnus was no longer sure he could afford the luxury of preserving Havard's life if he couldn't subdue him quickly.

Havard became his bear. Smaller than Magnus, but no less dangerous as he launched forward, jaws snapping at Magnus' face.

He jerked backward in time to avoid the sharp teeth, stumbling on the solid wood furniture tumbling under foot.

Under Havard's relentless offensive, Magnus swiped and batted away his face and claws again and again.

Tired and frustrated, Magnus rose on his hind legs and pounded Havard with his front paws, sending him flying into the opposite wall with a deafening crack.

Magnus roared at him to stay back.

Havard, dazed, stumbled to raise himself on all fours, shaking his head to clear it. He tottered for a moment, struggling to hold his balance.

Magnus dropped to plant his feet, preparing to either charge or divert Havard's attack when it came.

Both polar bears gripped their claws into the fine edges of the stone that made up the floor.

A roar from somewhere downstairs resounded throughout the castle, drawing Magnus' attention.

Elias!

No!

Magnus turned back in time to see Havard launch his entire body forward, jaw angled for his throat.

Pain shot through Magnus' neck muscles as Havard's teeth tore through the flesh and gripped him so hard, he inhibited his airflow.

Havard had him.

Havard tugged and slammed Magnus' head back against the stone wall.

Warm blood trickled down his back from the base of his skull to join the seeping gash across his shoulder. The blood flow from his haunch continued.

The roar resounded again, louder, closer.

Elias, putting himself in danger.

Ana could already be dead just beyond that door.

Deprived of air and weakened from loss of blood, his vision of the room narrowed, hazy and growing dark.

Magnus received the full force of Elias' third roar into Havard's face as he tightened his death grip on Magnus' throat.

The room went dark as Magnus sagged.

"Release him!" Elias' clear voice commanded. "Now!"

Havard growled, intent on fulfilling his duty.

"If my grandfather is dead, then I am your King. I command you to release your hold," he shouted, switching tactics.

Magnus' would have smiled if he could.

But he couldn't.

He drifted in the silence of the void.

I'M DEAD.

Nothing but blinding white light surrounded Analiese Maria Marguerita Francesca Ortega.

Her entire body tingled like she was wrapped in energized, raw cotton fluff.

"You're not dead. At least I don't think so," Antony's voice filled her head.

"Where are you?"

"I'm here, Ana, but you're encased in something... well, part of you is encased in something. Like Sascha was when she bilocated. Your body is unconscious and in the king's room."

She extended her hands. "I don't feel anything."

"I know you said you needed a priest, but Ana is the next best thing. If we can wake her up."

"Who are you talking to?"

"The shaman. He's not happy all these outsiders are invading the king's room."

"I'll bet," she murmured, turning in place, trying to discern something, anything that wasn't just more white space. Or cotton fluff. Or cloud haze—whatever *this* was. This certainly wasn't the same place Aksel was trapped in.

"The king is still alive, Ana, but just barely. The shaman is using his energy to keep him stable despite his resistance to the sigil."

"Is he in danger?" She peered in the distance, blinking. White on white movement. She drifted toward it.

"Not just yet. The bear woman and the magician are arguing over what to do while Magnus is fighting his way through the castle."

"Magnus?"

"Yeah, my god Ana, you picked a big bastard! I've never seen such an enormous bear in my life."

"Antony, you're a sailor. Have you ever seen *any* bears in your life?" she said, squinting into the light as the shape took form.

"That's besides the point. He's easily bigger than every other bear here. Anyway, we have to figure something out while this woman bear has her knickers in a panicked twist and is taking the other guy with her. Before they do something stupid."

"Okay," she murmured, full attention on the rounded figure that continued to move away.

"Okay? Listen to me. We can't break you out of this thing. It's hard as marble. You need to find a way out of it yourself."

"Oh, it's a bear!"

"What? Ana, are you listening to me?"

"Yeah, Antony, you can't break me out. There's a bear here. A white one. I feel like I should see where it goes."

She dimly registered a roar in the distance. But it wasn't coming from the white bear in her cotton fluff. It turned to look at her as she drew nearer. Its black eyes and nose were stark and glossy against the mass of white fur.

More roaring in the distance.

Ana was unconcerned.

Antony's insistent voice grew fainter as she followed the pristine polar bear away from all the noise.

A brush against her wrist drew her attention. Raising her hand, she stared at the garnet rosary her grandmother had insisted she keep. From it dangled both the crucifix and the carved polar bear the priestess had gifted her.

'When the light is blinding, the bear will guide you.' she'd said.

"Huh. Well, I'd say the light is blinding."

As she followed the bear, the quality of the light changed, allowing a bit of gray into the mass. Visible color striations pointed the way along a tunnel like structure.

Antony said I wasn't dead, and yet here I am going down a tunnel away from the light.

She studied the bear as they went, wondering if she could communicate with it as she had with Aksel in the astral.

Color drifted through the structure, mingling to form new colors, then drifted apart again. Threads of black also streaked through the mix of color and white and gray.

The bear stopped at a convergence in the tunnel where it branched off in several directions. The tingling she'd experienced in the white area intensified here, vibrating through her every particle, strongest along the center of her body from the crown of her head down to her pubic bone, reminding her of the Chakra diagram Jack had told her to memorize. Seven in all, with different functions and associated colors. Colors like those wisping through the mass surrounding her and the bear.

Ana turned toward the tunnel with more violet than any other color and stepped toward it.

The bear growled.

Ana blinked, returning her gaze to her guide. "Okay, not that way. Sorry." She turned her back on the attractive tunnel—and all the others drawing her attention—to focus on her designated direction.

The bear ambled down a greenish tunnel, which opened into a domed room. Not quite a dome, no... Ana squinted up into the ceiling. It was the roof of a cave covered in aurora borealis.

"So beautiful," she whispered, following the bear around a massive stalagmite. "But why am I here? What do I need to do?"

Beyond the stalagmite slumped a figure on the floor.

"Magnus!" Ana gasped, bringing her hands to her mouth.

Unconscious, he was naked and bleeding.

"Is he dying?" She rushed forward. She crouched, placing her hands on his face.

Next to her, the bear peered into his face, its expression so very sad.

"What do I do?"

The bear pressed its nose to Magnus' breastbone then poked Ana in the same place, shocking her by the gesture and the electric sensation. Her hand drifted to her chest.

Her heart.

Magnus' heart.

Her throat tightened. Instinct told her what the bear wanted her to do, but she couldn't form the words in her head.

Overhead, the lights shimmered green and blue.

Looking at the bear, she said, "I'm not sure I understand, but I'll try." The bear huffed and nudged her forward.

Ana straddled Magnus' thighs and sank to her knees.

Despite his weakened state, he radiated warmth.

With all her strength, she hooked her arms under his, leaning him toward her, chest to chest.

Heart to heart.

She closed her eyes. Listening to the beat of his heart and the beat of her heart.

In the magic of this place, it seemed to echo around them as they synced into a single beat.

Thoughts of one another had guided them together like a single pulsing polestar.

His hands slid around her waist and up her back as he nuzzled her shoulder. "Ana," his voice was hoarse as his arms crushed her to him. "I thought I'd lost you forever."

Enveloped in his embrace, she sank into him, eyes closed. "Not a chance, when you only just found me."

He pulled away just enough to look into her face.

It felt like a mile between them.

"What you said in the registrar's office?"

Mate.

"That I choose you?"

He nodded.

Emotion swelled her heart, making her throat constrict and her eyes tear up as her heart opened, responding to Magnus.

Love.

Acceptance.

That's all she'd ever wanted in her life, though she'd spent most of her time trying to bury that unrealistic longing.

In this place, somewhere outside of the reality they lived in, everything she felt was real. Everything that was in her heart, was real. It was all that mattered.

"For all time, Magnus." She took up his large hand and pressed his palm to her heart, and whispered. "For *all* time."

He pressed her palm first to his nose and lips, inhaling her scent, then to his heart, echoing her words. "I choose you for all time, Ana."

She brushed the tip of her nose across his.

He brushed his lips across hers.

They released each other's hands, and she reached for his face to deepen their kiss, while his arms wrapped around her waist and hips, pulling her impossibly close. He was naked beneath her, and his arousal was unmistakable.

She broke the kiss with a gasp, "Magnus, we're not alone—." Looking around the cave, the bear was gone.

They were indeed alone.

She looked into his eyes.

"Mate," she whispered. Instinct told her that this would be more binding than anything she'd ever committed to in her life.

"Do you want to finish this?"

"I want nothing more than to finish this," she said, quickly removing her clothes as a sense of impending urgency took over.

Undressing, here, was an act of deliberation in a place where they didn't actually have physical bodies.

They were all energy, co-mingling in this astral place—wherever it was.

All sensation and knowing and needing.

She resumed her place, straddling his thighs.

He slid an arm around her hips, pulling her close so that he could trail his lips over her heart.

She shuddered against the overwhelming sensation of emotion his tenderness elicited in her.

She slid her fiery core along his steely erection, then angled her hips so that his tip waited at her entrance.

Magnus claimed her lips, swiping his tongue along hers, teasing and enticing.

She moaned as need spiked through her. A need only Magnus could fulfill.

Ready, she drew him in, easing down his length.

Their breaths mingled as he filled her so that his tip rested against her sweet spot. Her toes curled against the intense pleasure.

Magnus grazed his teeth along the column of her throat, inhaling her scent and nibbling the tender skin until he reached the crook of her shoulder. With his forearm still encircling her hips, he pressed her down even further.

His breath hitched as he pulsed inside her.

She moaned his name as her hips tilted forward, then slid back.

Leaning against the support of his arm, she arched so that he had access to her breasts. As his mouth fastened on first one nipple and then the other, she rode him faster, harder still.

Magnus looked up into her face, reflecting her passion as they ascended.

He licked his lips. "You're sure, Ana? About the mating? It'll probably hurt."

As she looked into his eyes and saw her own vulnerability, she slowed her pace, rolling her hips.

She'd said forever, and that's what a mating was.

She'd spent enough time around shifters to understand that much, regardless of the mechanics.

"Yes," she breathed as her desire continued to ascend. "Yes, Magnus, I'm sure."

"Gods, I'll never get enough of you, Ana."

Tears gathered as her heart soared, opening to him. Those words sent her over the edge.

Too much.

"Magnus!" she warned; the colors in the room converged around them as she exploded. As her climax took her over, she gripped him, determined to take him with her.

Pain shot through the muscle at the crook of her shoulder. She dimly realized Magnus bit her as he joined her. It did nothing to detract from the rolling waves of ecstasy crashing through her.

TWENTY-SEVEN

"ANA! CAN YOU HEAR me, Ana?" Antony's voice boomed through Ana's consciousness.

"Yes, stop shouting." She groaned as energy continued to thrum through her while her shoulder throbbed with discomfort. She was back in the white space, the cave of coalescing colors nowhere to be seen.

This time, the texture to the place was different.

Internally, she felt different. The weight—no, the closedness—of her heart had lessened. Like her protective walls had crumbled away. It felt more open. Raw. Free.

"Ah thank God. I thought I'd lost you there for a minute."

"Only a minute?" She reached out, touching the film surrounding her.

I thought it was more like thirty...

"Yeah, you were talking about a bear, then just went quiet for a minute. I was freaking out here."

"Sorry," she murmured, fingers scratching at the film she'd been unable to see before, and pushed with her fingertip. It gave way like a dusty web coating an abandoned doorway.

Swiping at the clingy stuff, she cleared the way to step through into a room she'd never seen before, but instantly knew was the king's chamber.

And it was a busy place as she took in her new surroundings.

Antony stood to her immediate left, expression drawn in worry as he looked her over. At her feet lay her body, eyes closed and pale. Across from her body, she faced another mirror aspect of herself, which sent a shiver through her.

This is too weird. I really need to wake up.

You can't wake up yet, she said. Her other *self* pointed to an old man standing by the king's bedside.

The shaman.

He needs you to break the spell before the king dies.

Shouting drew Ana's focus to the other side of the room, where Elias stood inside the doorway facing his mother and her companion. Magnus lay unconscious at their feet, a blanket draped over him.

"That human needs to be imprisoned," Ulla Matochkin said to the guards beyond the room as she pointed at Ana's inert body on the floor. "We stopped her from assassinating the king for Magnus."

Ana laughed at the ridiculous accusation, drawing Yvan's attention.

He opened his mouth to speak when the shaman suddenly appeared in front of him. "Filth! Despoiler!"

Yvan grinned at the old man.

"What is so funny?" Elias demanded of the magician. "My grandfather is nearly dead, and my home is in chaos."

"Nothing, your highness," Yvan said to the prince, checking himself.

It must be done now, before it's too late. Ana's other *self,* pleaded with her. *I will help bridge you.*

"Shaman," Ana said, drawing the old man's attention. "I think I can help you."

With a final scowl at Yvan, he blinked forward, peering into Ana's face. She had no idea what he saw, but after a moment he searched the room, his gaze stopping at her twin before he nodded.

"What's going on?" Antony asked her.

"Seems my other *self* over there insists we can help the Shaman."

"Other self?" his eyes widened, looking around the room.

"You can't see her? The shaman can."

Yvan, watching the exchange, blanched. Again, he opened his mouth, lifting his hand toward Ana's body. He shouted two words when he was interrupted.

"Stop!" Elias commanded; eyes narrowed on the man with disgust. "There will be no conjuring in this room."

Ana's other *self* stepped forward, reaching out her hands toward Ana and the Shaman.

The shaman placed his hand in hers. Ana hesitated, looked up into the old man's eyes, and touched the proffered hand.

So many things happened all at once and none of them eased the uncomfortable sensations roiling through her body.

Yes, her body. The hard floor was distinct below her, the painted ceiling above her was breathtakingly beautiful and Antony's face was far too close to hers. Her hand lifted, shoving him away, but she wasn't controlling it or the rest of her as she struggled to her feet, head swimming.

God, I feel like I'm going to puke.

She reached for her head, but the other force occupying her body forced it away as her feet stomped her toward the king's bed.

"What's happening? What's wrong with her?" Elias demanded, eyes wide.

"Silence, young man!" The shaman barked through Ana's vocal chords.

Ana cringed, almost dislodging herself from her body.

Don't! Her other *Self* warned, also from within. *You agreed to do this. If you retract your will, the shaman won't be able to save the king or break the sigils.*

From the other side of the room Magnus groaned as he regained consciousness.

"Father!" Elias said, crouching down beside him.

"What's happening?" he rasped, rubbing his throat where Havard had nearly strangled him to death.

"I'm not sure, but I think your Ana is channeling the shaman."

The sensation of the shaman's being occupying her body wigged her out. "Antony, this feels so weird," she said as he stepped into the space beside her. She continued to resist the urge to shake the old man out as their beings seemed to vie for space, slipping against one another while trying not to force the other out.

Relax.

She tried. Truly she tried.

While she focused on that, the shaman continued his work.

"You don't know what she's doing. Why would she be channeling your dead shaman? She could be trying to finish what she started to ensure the king's demise," Yvan protested.

Elias moved so that he faced Yvan, scowling up into his face. "I know my shaman's voice when I hear it. Do not interfere."

Magnus stumbled to his feet. "He's worried that Ana and the Shaman will break his spell, releasing the control he and Wulker have over their victims. Including Aksel." He directed the last words at Ulla.

"Don't listen to his lies, Ulla. We'd never—*I'd* never do such a thing."

Ulla moved next to her son, holding Yvan's gaze. "Wouldn't you?"

Ana couldn't maintain her focus on the exchange any longer. Whatever the shaman was doing, he pulled her into it.

The old man chanted a Barentian song, hands extended over the King's head and torso. His soul's force drew power up through the soles of her feet, along her legs and into her heart where it churned around and around, making her feel like she had awe-inspiring heartburn.

The power gathering, combining with the emotion in her physical body, made her shake and tremble with possibility.

She was an open conduit to the Shaman's will as he pulled what he needed from the surrounding earth to boost the king's soul energy and keep him alive.

Next, Ana felt as though the shaman jack-knifed the power, swinging an extended right arm in Yvan's direction.

Hold on! Ana's other *self*—her *Higher Self* yelled as her grasp on Ana's and the Shaman's spirits tightened.

Yvan lurched toward the Shaman, chest first, as though dragged closer.

The tenor of the words changed as the Shaman's left hand hovered an inch above the black ink sigil marring his king's throat.

Yvan struggled against the invisible grip, grunting and crying out as though the Shaman was clawing something out of him.

The inked sigil appeared to burn off in layers until it streamed away, soaking into the king's pillow, leaving his skin clear again.

Once the sigil was gone from beneath the shaman's right hand, he swung it too, in Yvan's direction, an inch from his throat now. Chest arched out, throat pressed in, he struggled on tiptoe against the shaman's power, gasping.

"No. No. No!"

"You wish to steal and defile our sacred magics?" The shaman growled at the human magician.

Now, the energy of the Shaman's bear surged forward, snapping at Yvan with vengeance.

Its energy threatened to overpower Ana. Had it not been for the hold her *Higher Self* maintained on her, rooting her in her body as the Shaman exacted justice, she would have been consumed by it.

Ana snarled in Yvan's face as her fingers curled into claws, as though she held his heart in one hand, his throat in the other. She felt the rapid beat of his heart against her palm, the gush of air through his windpipe at her fingertips.

From her left palm, energy, white and hot, seared the skin of Yvan's throat. By the time she was done—the shaman was done. It scarred him with the same sigil, without the ink.

Instead of the octopus shifter's venom fueling the curse, Yvan's own power looped back into it, binding his will, containing any magic he had within his own body.

Done. The Shaman released his hold.

Yvan dropped to the floor at Ana's feet.

The room was silent except for her panting.

"Havard!" a guard outside the room shouted at the sound of another body dropping to the floor.

The shaman turned toward his king, and seeing that the king's breath came steady and strong in his still-unconscious state, he nodded, released his hold on Ana and stepped outside of her.

She collapsed to the floor.

"Oh god, I'm going to puke for real this time." She gagged, hand to her mouth, trying to contain herself.

Having tied the blanket around his hips, Magnus pulled Ana to her feet, crushing her to him. "What the fuck just happened?"

She couldn't draw enough breath to answer with her face mashed into his chest. Her arms encircled his waist, drawing comfort from his nearness.

The king groaned, and everyone turned their wide-eyed stares in his direction.

"Mngsf." Ana's muffled plea earned her instant release as Magnus peered down into her face.

His thumbs traced the bruises as he scowled. "I should rip them apart for this."

"Your highness, there are some outsiders requesting an audience in the great hall." A guard said, glancing between Elias and the King.

The king struggled to sit up.

Ulla rushed forward, "You shouldn't strain yourself—."

"Get away from me!" the king roared. To the same guard, he said, "Take this woman and detain her in her quarters. No one in or out until I decide what to do with her. And send someone to tend to our guests while I prepare."

"Yes, sir," the guard said, clearly shocked, as he reached for Ulla.

"Don't touch me!" she ripped her arm out of his grasp and marched out of the room. Yvan moved to follow her.

"Take that one downstairs with guards. If he tries to run away, maim him."

Ana scanned the room. Only the king, Magnus and the prince remained. The shaman and Antony looked on.

The shaman's curious stare made her uncomfortable. With a quick glance, she noticed that not only was her other *self* not visible, but that she felt solid. Whole in a way she never had before.

The shaman's wrinkled, tattooed faces split in a grin. "Even *more* enhanced human now."

She blinked, not understanding what that meant.

Beside her, Antony laughed.

"I'm going to check on my guys, Ana. I'll find you again soon." He was gone before she could respond.

She whispered to Magnus. "Should I wait outside while you talk to your father and son?"

"I'm going to hazard a guess that our outsider visitors belong to you." The king said to Ana and Magnus. "Am I right?" He turned to Elias.

Elias nodded. "Kane's team is here for you."

"Wulker?"

"They have him," Elias confirmed.

Tears sprang to Ana's eyes.

Magnus gripped her to him. "Then it's done."

She pulled away, smiling up into his face. "It's done."

He bent to press his lips to hers. "I will join you soon. Unless I'm to return to my cell." He glanced at the king over Ana's head.

"We have things to discuss," the king said, dismissing Ana.

Magnus nibbled her lips one final time, whispering, "I had one hell of a dream while I was unconscious."

Ana slipped out of his grasp, her fingers lingering in his as she moved toward the door. She slid her hand over the shoulder he'd bitten. "That wasn't a dream."

His eyes widened as she exited the room, closing the door behind her.

TWENTY-EIGHT

MAGNUS AND ELIAS HELPED the king dress.

He was weak from his long trial under the effects of the dark sigil.

"My old friend was keeping me alive from the otherworld," he'd said, matter of fact.

"I've no doubt. That was some dramatic possession he did of Father's mate. I've never seen anything like it," Elias said, awed, handing some of his grandfather's clothing to Magnus to dress in.

"Nor have I, and I certainly have no desire to see it again if I can help it," Magnus said, pulling on the trousers and shirt, happy to do away with the blanket.

The three men spoke with a hesitancy alien to each of them.

Three generations of polar bear royalty considered one another with uncertainty.

Finally, the king said to Magnus, "We will discuss our family matters at a later time. I revoke your banishment effective immediately. In the meantime, we must decide the fate of our prisoners." He placed a gentle hand on Elias' shoulder. "We will handle your mother's judgment ourselves. As a citizen of the polar bear community in Barentian territory."

"Before we go downstairs, I want to return something. It will only take a few minutes," Magnus said. Triggering the secret door, he slipped into the dark passageway to retrieve the objects he'd hidden there for safe-keeping.

As the bookshelf slid back into place, he handed the stone and the wrapped book to Bjorn. "I would have ensured that Elias received these if anything had happened."

Bjorn nodded, staring at the objects in his hands. "I know you would have." He unwrapped the book, smoothing a palm over the etched leather surface, then rolled the chunk of jet between his fingers.

"What are they?" Elias asked.

"These are the reason for our being here, Elias," Bjorn said, looking at Magnus. "The keys to something precious and sacred, and so dangerous we must protect it with our lives. They should have gone to your father for safekeeping on my death, along with the crown. But I know his destiny is elsewhere."

Magnus nodded. "It is. Since I'm no longer banished and intended for execution, I will continue to do all I can to uphold our family's duty from outside of Barentia."

Bjorn sighed. "We should have done things differently, perhaps."

"Perhaps. Or perhaps things went exactly as they were meant to."

Elias looked perplexed by the exchange.

"No matter, we have guests to see to." Bjorn laughed as he and Magnus replaced the items in their hiding places. "We will discuss these artifacts later."

Magnus opened the door to the antechamber to find the head guard still at his post.

Despite the other guards' insistence that Havard go to the infirmary, he stubbornly remained outside the King's chamber.

Battered and bruised from his battle with Magnus, who looked equally so, he also looked at the king with haunted eyes. "Sire, I—."

"I know," Bjorn Thornsson said to his chief guardsman.

It seemed to be enough.

Havard nodded his head and stepped aside to allow the King to continue on his way.

As they entered the throne room, the king signaled that they should move into the meeting room.

Relief flooded Magnus on seeing his entire team present, hale and whole. Ana laced her fingers through his as he stepped next to her.

Bjorn leveled his stern gaze on Magnus' team leader. "Kane. What do we have?"

"We have the suspect we've been seeking for over a decade in GPSA custody, thanks to your grandson and your people."

Bjorn raised a thick gray brow. "Explain."

Elias recounted his escape by boat and the call that brought Kane to the island. One transport helicopter went straight for the archipelago compound, while the other met with Elias and the Barentian villagers who had followed him in their fishing boats to Bear Island to ensure his safety. "As she flew us back, we saw the roving gangs engaging with the humans on this side of the channel. She refused to allow me to join them and brought me back here instead."

"As is right," Bjorn said.

"We've detained two ships, both bearing human cargo bound for the interior. Seems some of them were ready for us. They struck up a riot on our arrival."

"I didn't have to do much persuading," Raya said, grinning at Magnus. "Usually, I have to convince them I'm not a delusion, but these guys were eager."

"Naval crewmen?" Ana asked.

"Yeah."

"Emilio and the guys. They were Antony's men. From his ship when the accident happened."

Kane nodded. "We will contact the Navy."

"I want to know more about these outsiders that my daughter-in-law brought to my court. Her deception was great and deeply damaging. I know anything she confesses to will be shaded with denials and lies. She said one was her pet illusionist from her father's court and the other a business connection, also through her father's court."

"As far as we've been able to discover, that is true. But I also believe both men were members of *The Consortium*."

Magnus flinched as his father growled, turning away.

The Consortium.

And the human trafficking ring.

The two topics that had sundered his family.

"Wulker used his corporation to mask and grow his trafficking business. Ulla Matochkin gave him the protected base of operations he needed to function outside of international law. In your sovereign territory."

Bjorn's jaw worked as he listened, eyes glinting. He didn't interrupt.

Kane continued. "As for Yvan Putinovski." She shrugged. "My Deputy Director, Jack Maeda, has been studying the nature of the sigils used. They used Wulker's venom to create the sigil. But until we interrogate him, I can only theorize that his motive was access to your gate."

Bjorn went rigid, his gaze darting to the faces of Magnus' team.

"They're all trustworthy," Kane assured him.

The king turned his focus to Magnus.

Magnus nodded. "We're all dedicated to opposing *The Consortium*. And protecting this gate, as well as the others."

"Others? You've found them?"

"Not yet," Kane said quickly. "We're close to discovering the location of one, but it's painstaking work." The weariness in her demeanor was obvious despite her centuries of dedication. "With your permission, King Bjorn Thornsson, on behalf of the Global Paranormal Security Agency, we will remove the ships, perpetrators and all of their assets from your islands."

"Hm," he grunted, pursing his lips. "We will handle Ulla Matochkin ourselves."

"Thank you. And our GPSA medics report that Aksel Matochkin is awake and free of the same sigil. We will remand him into your custody as soon as he is well enough to travel."

Bjorn's brows rose. "I see. Good."

They said their goodbyes to the Barentians and made their way out to the transport helicopter, waiting to fly them to the trafficking compound.

On arriving, Kane went inside the main building to meet with the lead of the forensics crew.

Magnus and Ana hung back, staring at the place. Carson, Lirikai, Aaron, Raya, and Ian joined them. Perpetrators were clustered in one area with their wrists bound behind them, while victims gathered in another as GPSA prepared to transport them out of Barentian territory for the next steps.

"We did it," Carson said, shoulders relaxed.

"Now we can enjoy that vacation that keeps getting interrupted," Lirikai said, slipping her arm around Carson's waist.

He squeezed her to him, then looked at the rest of his team. "Vacation at my place?"

"I've never seen your island. As long as it's some place warm, I'm happy to crash," Ana grinned, her excitement clear.

Fingers linked, Raya looked up at Ian's quirked smile and said, "We'd be happy to join you."

"Perfect. Bring your apron, Ian. You're making us all scones." Mischief glinted in Carson's eyes. "Aaron?"

"I have some family matters I need to attend to back in Toronto, but yeah, I'll join for a few days."

"Awesome. We'll sort out the details later. Back to work, folks!" Carson tilted his head toward the activity and strode toward it. The others followed.

Ana pulled Magnus' fingers, hanging back.

He looked down into her concerned face and brushed his fingers over her creased brow, then along the discolored skin of her cheek and throat.

"This case ended, as I knew it would. Just not how I expected it should."

The corner of her mouth lifted. "Same here. I expected to be in Iceland."

"Disappointed? We could go there if you wish—."

Her forefinger shot up, pressing his lips together. "Hush! I wish for no such thing. I've had more than enough snow and ice and sub-zero temperatures for a lifetime."

He frowned as his heart sank. "You won't come back to Barentia?"

She searched his face and smiled. "I will. I recall you said you wanted many children. If we are so blessed, we will have to register them, won't we?"

He nodded as his heart buoyed again. "We will."

"Come on, you two, we have work to do," Carson called, hands cupped around his mouth.

Ana sighed. "I love him, I do..."

"Do you now?" Magnus lifted a brow.

"I do but not as much as I love you, I think." She poked his chest.

He threw his head back and laughed at the sky as he squeezed her close. "She thinks."

Ana rose on tiptoe to kiss Magnus.

He met her smiling lips with unspoken promises of their future.

With a final nibble, she broke the kiss, squeezed his hand, and said, "Let's go. The man says we have work to do."

EPILOGUE

THE SUN BLAZED AND Analiese Ortega basked in it like a contented cat, eyes closed, face upturned, worshipping the heat.

Stretched out on a lounge chair on Carson Perenga's tropical island terrace, she enjoyed vacation time with her GPSA teammates.

Carson's voice carried across the open space. "News from Pia Jensen."

Ana turned her head toward the sound of his voice without opening her eyes.

"I called to give her the news that we closed the case, since she helped us out in Montreal, which she was incredibly pleased about and sends her congratulations along with an open invitation to her wedding next summer."

Ana smiled, pleased by the news. The panther shifter was an excellent agent and deserved happiness.

"So, she and Renni Diaz decided to make it official. Good for them," Ian said with a grin. "Silky soccer skills, that one."

"Yeah, he's a good guy," Carson said.

Ana turned her attention away from the direction of their conversation as they continued talking about Renni Diaz's soccer career and the signed jersey he sent to Ian at Carson's request.

She sighed and adjusted her posture under her beloved sunshine.

A shadow loomed over her, interrupting her sunbathing.

She cracked an eye open to find Magnus' head blocking her heat source. "You look like a sun god with all that glowing blond hair flowing around your shoulders," she murmured, accepting the sweating glass of iced tea he'd brought her.

"And you're my bronzed goddess." He leaned down to kiss her before claiming the adjacent lounge chair. "How's your shoulder?" He reached out, grazing his fingers over the healing wound he'd inflicted while in the astral realm.

"It's fine, for the hundredth time."

"I still can't believe that was real."

"Any regrets?"

He scowled at her. "You know there aren't." His lips compressed as he sighed.

It was obvious to her that he wanted to say or ask her something.

She sat up, worried. "I've never seen you so hesitant. What is it, Magnus?"

He reached toward her again, his fingers trailing along her bare shoulder next to her bikini halter strap, and cleared his throat. "It's Barentian tradition for a priest or priestess to perform ritual body art on a mating mark. In our case, a shaman would do it."

"Oh," she said, rubbing a hand over her bare shoulder. She caught his fingers and squeezed, seeing how important the matter was to him. She dropped her gaze to his collection of beautifully drawn tattoos adorning his body. "And you think that would be... acceptable? For me to have such an honor?"

"If you like the idea..." he hedged.

"I do."

"Then yes, I do think it's acceptable. And I'd be honored that you would consider doing this."

Ana stood from her lounge chair and slid onto Magnus' lap, running her fingers through his loose hair. "Aside from the fact I'd do anything for you, I think it's a beautiful honor and look forward to having my first piece of body art created by a Barentian priest. How much more meaningful could that be?"

He cupped her face and claimed her mouth, expressing how important her acceptance of the matter was to him.

"We should go to our room," she murmured against his lips.

"We should." His muscles tensed to stand.

"We got a hit!" Joey Kane said from somewhere behind Ana, excitement in her voice.

Magnus rested his forehead against Ana's with a sigh, remaining as they were, but turned to give Kane their attention.

With her phone held aloft, Kane strode across the terrace, her swimsuit cover-up flowing around her slim legs.

"We've got a lead on a location for another gate!" she said again, eyes sparkling.

Ana smiled at her intense excitement. "That's great news, Joey."

"I've never seen her so animated," Magnus whispered. "And I've known Joey for a very long time."

Kane beamed. "Aaron called me with the information. I'm leaving in the morning to meet with him. When your time off is done, we'll convene and plan the next steps."

Ana breathed a sigh of relief and laughed. "I was worried you were going to send us all back this afternoon."

"Don't tempt me, Ortega," Kane said with a wink as she maintained her energetic stride and skipped back up the steps toward Carson's house, where Lirikai joined her.

"Let's go before anyone else has an announcement." Magnus set Ana on her feet, grabbed her hand, and tugged her toward the house.

Ana giggled, practically running to keep up with Magnus' long strides.

"Ana!" Raya called. "Ian's making scones soon if you want to join?"

"Not now!" Magnus growled, heading straight for their room.

"Maybe later," Ana called, laughing as she flew down the hall in Magnus' wake.

Pulling her into the room, he slammed the door shut and reached for Ana, intent on claiming her lips.

Magnus swooped her up into his arms, carried her to the bed, and lay her down without breaking the kiss. He pressed his body into hers and she wriggled beneath him, aligning his erection to her hot center.

Ana wrapped her legs around his clothed hips, drawing him closer.

His palm smoothed down her chest, over a breast, and continued on down her flat stomach. As his fingers hooked and tugged the band of her bikini bottom, his mouth slid along the same path, before finding her bellybutton.

"I'm going to worship you, Ana. Every inch." He nibbled the tender flesh just above her bikini band.

"If you insist," she moaned as his lips traveled lower, causing her to arch against him. "If you insist."

If you enjoyed the Aquatic Investigations trilogy in the Global Paranormal Security Agency series, check out:
Prowler, Cuffs & Claws Book 1

PROWLER

Relationships seem impossible when your secrets can cost you everything.

As an undercover GPSA agent, love and lust are high stakes risks that Pia Jensen prefers to avoid. But once Pia catches Renni's irresistible scent, her lonely inner kitty goes on the prowl.

Superstar Renni Diaz is at the pinnacle of his career when a hot little traffic cop pulls him over for speeding. Unable to keep her out of his mind, he knows that he's scored his heart's desire... even when she moves the goal posts on him.

After their first inevitable kiss, their 'no strings attached' relationship has a sizzling, fast-paced start.

When Pia's secret, and Renni's past, collide, they spiral down a path that compels them to choose between their growing love and the lives they had.

The Global Paranormal Security Agency

Please consider rating and reviewing **Polestar** on your favorite platform.

Read on for Chapter One of *Prowler*, a Global Paranormal Security Agency story...

PROWLER
CHAPTER ONE

Pia Jensen grunted as she thumbed past another text and tossed her phone on the passenger seat beside her.

Erin had just bailed on her, again.

Pia's squad lead, Tamara Cole, at the Global Paranormal Security Agency had encouraged her to integrate further with the Montreal police department she was embedded with, but she was only here for a couple more months, then she would be reassigned.

Mingle. Socialize. People.

The last year had been hard, and 'peopling' was very low on her list of priorities.

She missed her team. A team of kick-ass women GPSA agents. It was the one place where she'd finally felt like she belonged. And here, in Montreal, she was alone and still working solo. *Mostly* alone.

Her old friend and sometimes lover, Erin lived here but...she was busy with the chaos of running her club.

Pia sighed, swallowed some coffee from her favorite travel mug to lessen the sting, and acknowledged that this placement had been at her request.

For her dad.

She gulped more coffee, this time to bury the sharp rise of grief.

Her sensitive hearing picked up the growl of an expensive engine, gearing up. The speed radar triggered as a black sports car blew past her concealed location.

Time to go.

With a cursory glance for oncoming traffic, she threw the cruiser into drive, hit the gas, siren, and lights, speeding off in pursuit.

First thing in the morning, too.

These assholes in their tailored cars seemed to think speed limits were vague suggestions—simply inapplicable to them.

Probably another weaselly twenty-seven-year-old living off Mummy and Daddy's millions.

Following the car as it rolled to a stop on the hard shoulder, she killed the siren, then called in the license plate. She left the cruiser lights in their loop as she exited the car.

Pia sighed, putting her bitch face on, mentally prepared for some bullshit as she strode alongside the F-Type Jaguar, resisting the urge to trail a finger along its sleek fender.

The window eased down and a darkly tanned hand with long fingers extended identification details. The arm was encased in a crisp gray suit sleeve with working buttons. The cuff obscured the edges of black ink on the man's skin. An Aikon glinted in the sunlight. Bergamot and black pepper tickled her sensitive nose as his aftershave, mingled with the undertone of his personal scent, drifted toward her on the morning breeze.

Human.

Her inner kitty's attention was piqued.

"Good morning, sir." Fingertips resting on her hips, she took the last step up to the window, ignoring the proffered identification. "Are you aware we have speed limits in this city?"

"Yes. I'm late for work." Shadows obscured the driver's profile, with his face turned away as he scrolled through messages on his phone.

She didn't miss the Spanish accent.

Pia's teeth ground. Arrogant prick wasn't even deigning to pay attention to her.

"Late for work or not, you were driving thirty kilometers over the limit for this zone. There are kids and seniors that have places to go, too," she said, doubting her point would have any affect.

He put his phone down and turned to look up at her.

Had she stopped breathing? Damn... *Damn*! She knew that face. It adorned a thirty-foot banner next to the front doors outside the local soccer stadium.

Renni 'The Pitch Prowler' Diaz.

Her stomach quivered.

The tickets in her locker at the station were for the derby that night. Both of Montreal's professional soccer teams would be going head-to-head. He was expected to appear on the starting lineup. The growing rivalry between the teams promised excitement on the field. She'd been looking forward to this game, all week.

And he was so *damned* hot.

She steeled herself against the fan girl excitement gathering in her stomach, threatening to erupt in a juvenile giggle.

Her eyes drank in the view for a moment. That mouth. She'd fantasized about those lips, many nights.

"Yeah, listen, I really am in a hurry after a meeting that ran late this morning. Can we just call it a warning and I'll be on my way? I promise to be mindful in the future," he said, tossing her a grin.

Pia straightened. "I see." Disappointment steamrolled her as she pulled her pen and pad from its place on her vest, taking her time. Plucking the cards from his still-extended hand, she began to fill out the speeding ticket.

"Do you like sports?" He turned his wrist, glancing at his watch. "I can get you tickets to tonight's soccer match. Bring a friend?"

Her eyes flicked up from her pad, just having written his name. Renni Diaz. His address told her he'd been coming from home, heading for the training facility. After being embedded with local law enforcement for the last year, she was getting to know the city districts well enough.

"Already going," she grunted.

"Ah wonderful. Perhaps we'll see each other later tonight." He let his gaze sweep her from head to hip, before resting on her face, brow quirking.

Was he seriously trying to flirt his way out of a ticket?

It wasn't like he couldn't afford to pay it...

Image.

Speeding tickets didn't look good on a high-profile personality's image.

She shrugged. Not her problem.

She finished writing up the ticket, handing it to him. "Good luck tonight." She turned, stepping toward her cruiser.

His fingers ghosted hers as he accepted the slip of paper. "Will I see you after the game..." He glanced at the ticket. "Constable Jensen?"

Glancing back, she quirked a brow, ignoring the shiver caused by his touch. "I will be joining some friends for drinks downtown."

If Erin didn't bail on that too.

He squinted at her, considering. "L'Auberge, Dominion or Chatton Noir?"

That was a pretty specific short list. "Chatton Noir," she said, surprised.

"I have friends on the force, too." He grinned again.

"Have a good day." She dismissed him, again turning toward her cruiser.

"I'll see you tonight," he said as he pulled away from the curb, resuming his drive. At the stop sign, he gunned the engine a couple of times, pulling her attention to see if he was going to speed away.

He didn't.

Instead, he waved and turned the corner.

Weird.

She dropped back into the driver's seat of her cruiser with a snort.

She couldn't help pondering the image he'd conjured of meeting her at the bar later.

Bullshit.

Too bad; it dulled the shine of her fantasy of him a little.

Except for how hot he was. So much better in person. And he smelled amazing.

A guy like that wasn't going to just show up at a pub looking for her.

With a grunt, she dismissed that train of thought and put her cruiser into gear.

Back to work.

READ MORE OF PROWLER AT:
https://jodikendrick.com/book/prowler/

Thank You!

Dear Reader,

Thank you so much for taking the time to read *Ana Ortega* and *Magnus Bjornson*'s story in **Polestar**!

The **Global Paranormal Security Agency (GPSA)** journey started with my first book **Awakened**, featuring *Carson Perenga* and *Lirikai of the Barra'kidai.* This is where we first meet Ana, when she requests Carson's presence for a mysterious murder case on the West Coast.

The crew meet *Raya Burns* and *Ian McLachlan* in **Surfacing**, book two of the **Aquatic Investigations** trilogy when Carson, Lirikai and Ana track their suspects to the East Coast.

Carson and Lirikai appear in **Prowler**, the first book of the **Cuffs & Claws** series which features *Pia Jensen* and *Renni Diaz*. They also work with the dragon shifters of the **Dragon Island** series in **Dragon Heat** and **Dragon Steel**.

I hope you enjoyed **Polestar** and are interested in reading more of my work.

Please consider leaving a review on your favorite platform.

~Jodi

ABOUT JODI KENDRICK

Jodi Kendrick lives in Eastern Ontario Canada with her *Favourite Person* and chompy furbaby, while their adult children explore the wider world.

As a romance author, she writes in paranormal, fantasy, steampunk & gaslamp subgenres, and sometimes delves into urban fantasy and paranormal women's fiction. Her characters are often quirky, sometimes cranky, but they all woman-up and get the job done while their partners ensure they survive with all their bits and bobs attached.

A history enthusiast and word dabbler most of her life, she enjoys exploring 'beyond-the-everyday' and the 'time-before-now', discovering relationship threads weaving individuals through time and place. She's rarely seen without flashy notebooks and colourful pens.

Follow Jodi on Social Media:

Dragon Island
Dragon Heat

Enchanted Ardor
Wish

EveL Worlds : FUCN'A
Tough Nut
Diamond in the Ruff
Honeyed Nut
Gorilla in the Hiss
FUCN'A Collection One
Pedigree Collection

Finely Aged
Dragon Steel

Global Paranormal
Security Agency
Awakened
Surfacing
Polestar
Aquatic Investigations
Prowler

The Kindred Chronicles
Healer
Mercenary

The Soaring Dragon Chronicles
Return Flight
Changeling